Hunter Wolfe didn't come to her at night, he didn't come in the early morning, he didn't suddenly appear during the daylight hours....

Hannah missed him so much her teeth hurt. Every bone in her body ached for him.

This separation was a good thing, she kept telling herself. It meant that Hunter was adjusting to new circumstances without any problems. It meant he could resume his life and she could resume hers.

But, oh...she missed the totally uninhibited man who expressed his every emotion whenever it occurred. She missed the almost savage, who heeded the call of the wild, the pull of the moon.

The Hunter she knew and loved was a force of nature. Had she tamed him too much?

Dear Reader,

April may bring showers, but it also brings in a fabulous new batch of books from Silhouette Special Edition! This month treat yourself to the beginning of a brand-new exciting royal continuity, CROWN AND GLORY. We get the regal ball rolling with Laurie Paige's delightful tale *The Princess Is Pregnant!* This romance is fair to bursting with passion and other temptations.

I'm pleased to offer *The Groom's Stand-In* by Gina Wilkins— a fascinating story that is sure to keep readers on the edge of their seats…and warm their hearts in the process. Peggy Webb is no stranger herself to heartwarming romance with the next installment of her miniseries THE WESTMORELAND DIARIES. In *Force of Nature,* a beautiful photojournalist encounters a primitive man in the wilderness and must find a way to tame his oh-so-wild heart.

In *The Man in Charge*, Judith Lyons gives us a tender reunion romance where an endangered chancellor's daughter finds herself being guarded by the man she's never been able to forget—a rugged mercenary who's about to learn he's the father of their child! And in Wendy Warren's new sensation *Dakota Bride*, readers will relish the theme of learning to love again, as a young widow dreams of love and marriage with a handsome stranger. In addition, you'll find an intriguing case of mistaken identity in Jane Toombs's *Trouble in Tourmaline*, where a world-weary lawyer takes a breather from his fast-paced life and finds his sights brightened by a lovely psychologist, who takes him for a gardener. You won't want to put this story down!

So kick back and enjoy the fantasy of falling in love, and be sure to return next month for another winning selection of emotionally satisfying and uplifting stories of love, life and family!

Best,

Karen Taylor Richman
Senior Editor

Please address questions and book requests to:
Silhouette Reader Service
U.S.: 3010 Walden Ave., P.O. Box 1325, Buffalo, NY 14269
Canadian: P.O. Box 609, Fort Erie, Ont. L2A 5X3

Force of Nature

PEGGY WEBB

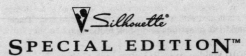

SPECIAL EDITION™

Published by Silhouette Books

America's Publisher of Contemporary Romance

For Michael...forever

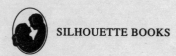 SILHOUETTE BOOKS

ISBN 0-373-24461-4

FORCE OF NATURE

Copyright © 2002 by Peggy Webb

This edition published by arrangement with Harlequin Books S.A.

Visit Silhouette at www.eHarlequin.com

Printed in U.S.A.

Books by Peggy Webb

PEGGY WEBB

and her two chocolate Labs live in a hundred-year-old house not far from the farm where she grew up. "A farm is a wonderful place for dreaming," she says. "I used to sit in the hayloft and dream of being a writer." Now, with two grown children and more than forty-five romance novels to her credit, the former English teacher confesses she's still a hopeless romantic and loves to create the happy endings her readers love so well.

When she isn't writing, she can be found at her piano playing blues and jazz, or in one of her gardens planting flowers. A believer in the idea that a person should never stand still, Peggy recently taught herself carpentry.

Dear Hannah,

What a celebration life has been! Your father finally came out of his coma after six months of tears and prayers. I feel as if I am discovering love for the first time. However, it is you that I worry about— my most passionate child.

I always knew that it would take a strong man to capture your heart. Therefore, when you met Hunter I sensed that you had found true love. I could hear it in your voice when you called me from Alaska. Just as with everything else you do, you put your heart and soul into that man—bringing him back from the wilderness, reintroducing him to civilization—but you cannot force him to stay. Do not be afraid to speak your heart. Tell him you love him, Hannah. If the feelings between the two of you are real, he will return. He will find his way home.

My heart goes out to you,

Mom

Chapter One

From the diary of Anne Beaufort Westmoreland:

October 20, 2001

The mountain changed everything for me. I'm not talking about Michael's coma; I'm not talking about that awful day four months ago when an avalanche crashed over my husband and put him in this deep sleep.

I'm talking about Jake and Emily's wedding on Mount Everest. I don't know what happened there in the Himalayas, but I came back a different woman. More courageous, somehow. More hopeful. Infused with the lightness of being.

When I got back to Vicksburg the first thing I did was hurry to the nursing home so I could visit my husband. This is the odd thing. I didn't go expecting a miracle. I didn't set myself up for the same big letdown I've experienced every day for the last few months. Instead, I went with the absolute certainty that everything is going to be all right.

No matter what.

There, now. I've said it. Even if Michael never wakes up, even if he never returns to me, everything is going to be all right.

Perhaps this is the miracle I've been waiting for, this great change in myself, this sense that I've been freed from the mundane and can now live my life on a higher plane.

Right now I don't know exactly what that means, but I'm going to find out. Clarice reads that kind of stuff all the time. I'll ask her for some books. I'll concentrate on living my life the best way I know how. Maybe that's exactly what Michael needs—time and space to work his own way back to me. Maybe he hasn't come back yet because I've been pushing too hard, expecting too much.

As soon as I finish this diary entry I'm going to lie down beside him and hug him and kiss him and say, Darling, just take your time. Come back when you're ready. I'm here loving you. I will always love you.

There. I feel better already. Lighter. More hopeful.

Now I can concentrate on other things. My gardens. My friends. My children.

Daniel and Skylar are already talking about having the family's Thanksgiving dinner at their house. They mentioned it before I left the Himalayas.

Well, why not? It would be selfish of me to insist that we gather at Belle Rose the way we always have, especially since I don't know whether Michael will still be in his deep sleep.

Besides, with two of my children married and one off in the wilds of Alaska, things are different now. Daniel didn't say so, but I have a feeling Skylar needs to play hostess to the Westmoreland clan in order to cement her place in this family.

And anything goes with Emily. Of all my children, she has always been the easiest. When she and Jake return from their honeymoon I'll just say, "Em, we're having Thanksgiving in Atlanta with Daniel," and she'll say, "That's great, Mom."

Hannah, of course, would have an opinion. But my oldest child is in Denali National Park chasing another story, and I won't be hearing from her unless there's an emergency. She's that much like Michael. Totally dedicated to her work. Totally committed to being the best photojournalist there is. Both of them have tunnel vision when it comes to their careers.

There I go again. Talking about Michael as if nothing has changed.

Everything has changed. Except my love. And that will never, ever change. Michael is my soul, my heart, my life, and I will always love him. No matter where he is.

Chapter Two

Something was out there watching her. Hannah pondered whether to get up and shine her flashlight into the darkness so she could see what it was or to stay inside her tent where she was safe…unless the intruder was human. And bent on mischief.

She eased her hand out of her sleeping bag and closed it over the butt of her rifle. She'd never used it to defend herself, but she could if she had to. Anyone who had read articles with Hannah Westmoreland's byline understood that she'd gone into some of the world's most remote and dangerous places to find the story. It would be foolish to go unprepared.

She lay still, waiting and listening. In the week since she'd been in Alaska following the trail of the wolf, she'd had many encounters with other wildlife, including a brown bear. But not a grizzly. She hadn't even seen one from a distance, and she certainly didn't relish the idea of seeing one at close range.

The skin at the back of her neck prickled. Her watcher was still there.

An animal would have satisfied his curiosity and moved on. All her instincts told Hannah her watcher was not an animal.

She had no intention of being caught by surprise, trapped inside the folds of her sleeping bag. Gripping her gun, she eased forward and peered through the crack where her tent flap was secured.

A full moon silvered the wings of her twin-engine plane and the snow that had dusted the campsite while she slept. The primeval beauty caught her high up under the breast-bone, and it was a moment before she made out the shadow underneath a giant black spruce tree.

It was a lone wolf. Majestic. Powerful.

His head swiveled toward the tent and he looked right at her. Hannah's heart hammered so hard she thought the wolf must have heard. There was something about his eyes gleaming in the moonlight, something almost human.

Her instincts kicked into high gear. *There's danger here,* they were saying, and yet she felt no fear.

Suddenly the wolf tilted his head upward and sent a cry to the moon that chilled Hannah's spine. It wasn't a howl so much as a gut-wrenching sound of agony. A plea.

And why not? Man seemed determined to wipe the wolf off the face of the earth.

That was why she was in Denali: to capture the wolf on film and present him to the public as a noble creature. Not the dangerous predator many believed, and certainly not vermin in need of extinction.

She thought of the wolves she'd been following the past week and how she'd seen two of them cavorting together in the sun, the male biting the muzzle of the female to show his affection. She'd watched as they disappeared into the deep woods, Adam and Eve in possession of Eden.

And she'd understood why they roamed the great woods and why she would do everything in her power to protect them.

Now she loosened her grip on the gun and studied her watcher. He was much larger than the wolves she'd photographed. The largest she'd ever seen. In fact, he was off the wolf-scale in size.

Furthermore he was alone, which defied everything she'd read about wolves. They were sociable animals who traveled in packs.

Was this wolf an outcast? An outlaw?

He lowered his massive head and studied her once more. A shiver shook Hannah, but not from the cold. Not at all from the cold. She wrapped her arms around herself in order to hold still. She didn't want any sound, any movement to drive her watcher away.

This creature was magnificent. Why hadn't she reached for her camera instead of her gun? Could she get it without alerting him?

As she crept backward, crablike, Hannah suppressed a giggle. Nothing majestic about her. Ridiculous would be a better description. She was armed against the cold with long thermal underwear and ugly flannel pajamas that she was going to burn as soon as she returned to Mississippi.

Why hadn't she flip-flopped her assignments and gone to the jungle in the fall and the frozen northwest in the summer? Then she could have been stretched out on a blanket letting the stars kiss her naked skin.

Her mother had often told her she had the instincts of a wild animal and the cravings, to boot. Hannah guessed that was so. Why else did she spend so much time in jungles and forests and mountains? She could have followed stories that took her to glamorous places, big cities and bright lights.

Why was she here in Denali at the onset of winter?

Passion, her mother always said. *Hannah is full of passion.* And Hannah knew it was so. She brought such intensity to her work that after she turned in a story she was drained.

What would happen if she ever met someone she could love? Someone who would love her right back? Would the intensity burn her up like a comet?

Hannah shook her head, disgusted with herself. All those weddings had her addlepated. First her sister, then her brother.

Let them follow the straight path. Tradition wasn't for her. Hannah would always choose the back roads, destination unknown.

Her hand closed around her camera, and she inched her way back to the tent flap to train her lens on the wolf. He was still in shadow and a cloud had passed over the moon. Hannah bided her time. This one was worth waiting for.

She adjusted the focus and had zoomed in for a close-up when suddenly the moon popped from behind the cloud. Hannah froze. That was no wolf...that long tangle of hair, those eyes.

But what then? What?

The click of her shutter startled the creature and he loped into the woods. She strained her eyes toward the woods, looking for a sign, a shadow.

And even though she could no longer see him, she knew he still watched. Somewhere out there in the darkness.

Hannah dressed at first light, and when she stepped outside, big drops of rain splatted at her feet. She shook her fist at the sky.

"Don't you dare rain until I check those tracks."

She raced in the direction she thought she'd seen the creature and studied the ground. Nothing. Not even the criss-cross tracks of mice and birds.

Hannah scanned her campsite. Everything looked different in the daylight. Where had she seen him? Which direction? Which tree?

"Think," she said. "Think."

Her habit of talking to herself came from years of traveling alone, chasing her stories solo and often hearing no voice except her own for weeks at a time.

Something was whispering to her. Instinct. Angels. Something.

She turned around and saw the giant spruce, and suddenly she knew that was where she'd seen him. The creature of the night. The powerful watcher who exuded danger without making her afraid.

Hannah hurried to the tree, careful as she came closer not to step over any tracks.

There. Near the trunk. Protected by the thick branches.

Hannah knelt to get a closer look…and there in the new-fallen snow was the footprint of man.

"It can't be. It can't possibly be true."

She'd seen a wolf. Hadn't she?

She got down on all fours and searched for more tracks. Indecipherable indentions were scattered about, but the rain had wiped out any further evidence of the creature who had watched her from afar.

Was her mind playing tricks? Had she seen what she'd thought?

Hannah turned back to study the track. It was still there, undisturbed. Awestruck, she eased her own boot into the track. Though she was a tall woman with a long foot to match, the footprint in the snow dwarfed her boot.

Was her watcher man or beast? She had no idea, but she intended to find out. Hannah raced to the tent to get her rain slicker and her camera then began to climb upward in the direction he'd gone.

It didn't take her long to realize the path was leading back to the territory of the wolf pack she'd been following for days. Up ahead she saw the outcropping of rock where the females sometimes sunned themselves while their cubs wrestled nearby.

Their den was in the vicinity. Yesterday she'd gotten close enough to see the mouth of the cave. They probably didn't trust her, but at least they were no longer afraid of her.

Today not a wolf was in sight, not even the enormous white alpha male who protected his pack. Hannah pulled up the hood of her rain slicker and hunched down on a big rock to wait.

Nothing stirred except the wind, which had picked up speed. The rain pelted down harder. Even if she saw something, she could no longer get a clear shot.

Besides, she hadn't packed any food and she was getting hungry.

Hannah turned to go when a prickle along the back of her neck alerted her. With slow and deliberate movements she swiveled toward a thick stand of firs only a dozen feet away. And there in the shadows was her watcher.

He could be no other. His size alone gave him away. In the daylight he looked enormous. Through the curtain of rain she saw that what she had mistaken for a wolf's coat was actually the skin of some larger animal— Perhaps a bear with the head gone.

And the hair...Hannah strained her eyes through the

mists. The thick tangle of hair was sun-streaked and long. But it was the eyes that mesmerized Hannah. Pale and glowing. Even from a distance they held her spellbound.

They stared at each other—Hannah and the wolfman. She saw curiosity in his eyes. Intelligence. And something else. Something she couldn't define. Something that made her pulse hammer and her mouth go dry.

Could she risk one quick shot without driving him away?

Maybe…if she could ease the camera into position on the rock and shoot blind. And if the rain would cover the sound of the shutter clicking.

Hannah eased her hand onto her camera and clicked. Once. Twice. Three times.

Either he didn't hear or whatever enthralled him overcame his natural desire to flee. The rain abated and still his gaze was on her, unwavering and extraordinarily disturbing.

The temperature had risen since morning and her slicker created a sauna-like effect. Hannah felt too hot…and it had nothing to do with the weather. She couldn't take her gaze off the wolfman. She'd never seen eyes like his. The softest gray so luminescent they looked silver.

Could she capture his eyes on film? Could she change to a zoom lens without disturbing him?

Still watching her watcher, Hannah made the adjustments. There now. It was done. But could she get the shot without focusing?

No. She'd have to aim and shoot. And risk losing him.

But the prize was worth the risk. If she worked quickly enough she'd have a close-up head shot of a real wolfman.

Her hand moved to the camera, and then she had second thoughts. This was not a wolf, but a man, and she was fully exposed with no protection. What if she made him angry? What if he came after her?

He might come after her anyway. It would soon be dark, and who knew what would happen then?

She could see the headlines: Photojournalist Mauled In Alaska. She couldn't do that to her mother. Not on the heels of her father's accident.

Trying to act naturally, Hannah picked up her camera and started back to her campsite. Out of the corner of her eye she could see the wolfman still standing in the shadows.

Good. That meant he wasn't following her.

Maybe the sun would shine tomorrow and she could come back into the rocky terrain and get some good footage. Evidence to back up her story. Proof that her mind wasn't deceiving her, that working alone for so many years hadn't driven her around the bend.

Back at camp she ate some jerky then built a big fire, stripped and sat huddled over it wrapped in a blanket.

"This feels so good," she said, then stretched her feet and hands toward the flames, and her blanket slid to the ground.

She'd reached to pull it back when the nape of her neck prickled. Hannah looked up, and there crouched at the edge of the woods in the gathering dusk was the wolfman, his silvery eyes gleaming in a predatory way that had nothing whatsoever to do with the hunt for food.

She couldn't breathe, couldn't move. She stared into those mesmerizing eyes while small details filtered through her trance—his jaw, square and powerful; his nose, somewhat crooked as if it had been broken many times, but nonetheless fine, even aristocratic; his lips, wide and sensual. Wet. Intoxicating.

Heat seared through Hannah, and she became aware of her own condition—skin sensitized as if hands caressed her, breasts tight and heavy-feeling, nipples fully aroused. She thought she might explode. She had to have relief.

Her hands moving downward were not connected to her body. The wet heat she encountered was separate from reality. The cry that escaped her was not her own.

The only thing real was the creature who watched her. Man or beast. She didn't care. She was a prisoner of passion so primal it stole reason, a willing captive of the wild wolfman who watched from the woods.

Chapter Three

As soon as it was light enough to see, Hannah hiked to the one place she knew her cell phone would work, the top of the hill above her camp. Every step of the way she second-guessed herself. Should she call her editor or not? No doubt she'd stumbled onto the biggest story of her career, and yet she couldn't think of the wolfman as a *story*. When she thought of him—which was constantly—she imagined him in much more personal terms.

Last night they'd shared an odd intimacy, Hannah by the fire and the savage creature in the woods. More intimate than anything she'd ever known. What had happened had forever changed her relationship with the wolfman, and now she found herself in the untenable position of uncertainty.

Hannah didn't like to think of herself that way. It made her uncomfortable. Decisiveness suited her. Boldness.

Only one obstacle stood between her and the pinnacle…a

huge boulder that blocked the path. As she climbed over it she became aware that she was not alone. Every nerve in her body went on alert. Somewhere out there, deep in the shadows of the forest, the wolfman watched.

Hannah didn't look for him until she'd reached the top. Shading her eyes against the sun, she scanned the deep woods. Nothing stirred. Not so much as a leaf. Still, she knew he was there. All her instincts warned her.

Her heart hammered hard; her imagination caught fire. And her body. Such primitive urges overtook Hannah that she suppressed a groan.

She'd been too long in the woods. That had to be it. She needed to dispatch her story and hurry to civilization.

Turning her back on the tall spruces, the massive ferns and the towering mountain peaks, she dialed the number of the magazine, *The World's Wild Places.*

Her editor answered. "Jack," she said. "Can you hear me?"

"Loud and clear. What's up, Hannah?"

She thought of the wild man watching her from the woods. Listening. Could he understand?

"Hannah? Are you there?"

"I'm here." She had to make a decision. She could give her editor some excuse about updating her original story. Hannah squinted into the deep woods, searching for answers. "How's Jessie?"

Jack snorted. "She's great. Hannah, cut the bull. You didn't call to ask about my wife."

"No...there's some kind of primitive man in the woods watching me, Jack. At first I thought he was a wolf..."

"My God, Hannah. Do you have your rifle?"

"No. The climb up here is too steep."

"Dammit..."

"He's not going to harm me, Jack. He's curious, that's all."

Was it? She thought of the way he'd looked at her across the firelight. That hadn't been curiosity in his eyes, but pure primitive desire.

"Follow him," Jack told her. "Get all the footage you can and call me tomorrow. I'll see what I can find out...and Hannah, be careful."

Following the wolfman was easy. Too easy. Was he leading her into a trap?

Hannah shifted her backpack, dropped to the ground and propped her back against the trunk of a black spruce. No need to leave herself fully exposed. She could no longer see her quarry, but she knew he was out there.

She reloaded her camera. Not that it would do any good. In the last few hours she'd taken plenty of shots, but not a single one revealed anything that would excite a reader. The wolfman had made certain of that.

He'd toyed with Hannah all day, revealing himself just long enough for her to raise the camera, then vanishing so quickly she ended up with nothing but a glimpse of his fur-covered arm or a fleeting view of his fur-covered back. Nothing that would identify him as a man clad entirely in bearskin and crude boots lashed high on his legs.

Hannah slung her camera over her shoulder then pulled out some strips of beef jerky. Across the clearing the branches suddenly parted and the wolfman emerged. Full frontal view.

If she reached for her camera he would vanish. No need to waste her time. Instead she held up the beef jerky.

"This is good. Do you want some?"

He tilted his head to one side, the movement fluid, graceful. He was standing as he had been near the entrance to the wolves' den, perhaps imitating her, perhaps not. There was keen intelligence in his eyes. Through the years he had no doubt learned that his body was made for being upright, that he could move faster that way than on all fours.

Hannah chewed her meat, watching him watching her. She smiled. "Come over here and join me. I won't hurt you. See?" She stretched her hands toward him, palms up in the age-old gesture of peace.

He didn't move, didn't make a sound, merely watched her with eyes that were strangely beautiful and powerfully disturbing.

She wasn't hungry, but she forced herself to eat. Hiking the mountain trails took stamina. Still watching the wolf-man, she placed one piece of beef jerky on the upthrust root of the spruce.

"This is for you." She gestured as she talked. Did he understand anything she was saying? He gave no indication. Instead he held her captive in a steady burning gaze.

Hannah turned away, shivering. It was time to move on.

"Let's go," she said. "You lead, I'll follow."

The wolfman vanished into the woods. He was gone so quickly Hannah couldn't even see the branches move. Which way had he gone?

Upward, she guessed. She glanced back at the spruce tree to get her bearings and that's when she noticed that the jerky she'd left on the tree root was gone. She hadn't seen a thing. How had he done that?

Furthermore, she was losing her bearings. When she'd first started following the wolfman she'd known exactly how to get back to her camp. Then it seemed he'd led her in circles, deeper and deeper into the woods. Soon she'd have to make a decision: return to camp while she still knew the way or continue following him.

But how could she follow him when she could no longer see him?

"Where are you?" There was no response. Not even a breeze stirred the branches above her. "Please come back. I need you."

He materialized so fast she jumped back. The wolfman was less than ten feet from her, and she would swear there was a twinkle of humor in his eyes.

She covered her heart with her hand, laughing.

"Don't do that to me. You scared me half to death."

Was that a smile? The expression was so fleeting she couldn't be sure. Besides, he was moving rapidly now, not even glancing backward to see if she followed. Even if she hadn't been making as much noise as a cow caught in a briar patch she knew that he would *know*. Years of living wild would have honed his senses to a keenness rivaling that of the wolf.

After half an hour Hannah found herself struggling to keep up. She was just getting ready to complain when he stopped on a high outcropping of rock and waited for her.

Did he read minds, too? That made twice in the last four hours he'd stopped to wait for her. It also added to the anecdotal evidence she'd collected that animals have a highly developed telepathic ability. Though he was no animal. Of that, she was all too aware.

She was getting ready to say, *Let's go,* when he surged ahead. When Hannah realized where he was taking her, she laughed. He had led her on a five-hour tour only to arrive at the site of the wolves' den less than an hour's hike from her campsite.

Had he been toying with her? Testing her stamina? Testing her loyalty?

He was standing near the entrance to the cave, watching her.

"What now?" Hannah asked. "What do you want?"

He retreated a few paces, then moved toward the cave once more. The sun glistened on the skins he wore and on his gold-streaked hair. He looked like a god from the ancient myths—powerful, sensual and completely irresistible.

"Is that your cave? Is that what you're trying to tell me?"

He ducked inside and the darkness swallowed him. Following him would be madness.

"No," she said. "I won't go in there."

He reappeared and blocked the entrance. The way he stared at her was so compelling she felt as if invisible strings were tugging at her. *The call of the wild,* she thought, and then she became almost hysterical, for suddenly she realized why he had led her all day long.

It was part of the wolf's mating ritual. Males left the pack to seek a mate. Once they found her, they led her through the forest until they could find a spot suitable for forming their own pack.

Hannah's face burned as she thought of their encounter by firelight. The same urgent feelings were coursing through her now, and for one crazy moment she thought about casting her backpack aside and following this amazing primitive man into his lair.

Suddenly his head came up and his nostrils flared.

"Great," she said. "Now I'm giving off come-and-get-me signals."

Never taking his eyes from hers, he tossed his long hair.

"No." Her voice was so soft she could hardly hear herself. "Not that I'm not tempted. Lord, you'd be out of that bearskin in a minute if you knew how much I'm tempted."

So tempted that she'd forgotten her purpose. *Pictures.*

No sooner had she thought the word than the wolfman vanished. Not into the cave but into the brush nearby.

She had her camera up and shooting, but the only thing she captured was the tangled undergrowth as it closed behind him.

She waited for him until the sun started sinking, and then she hurried back to her camp. He didn't follow her. If he had, she would know. That's how attuned she was to him.

She stowed her gear, ate beans from the can then wrapped herself in a blanket and sat in front of her fire, still thinking of him.

And suddenly he was there, deep in the shadows watching her. She could feel his eyes on her, feel how her skin tingled and her breath shortened and her heart hammered.

Langor overtook her…and the familiar liquid heat.

"I will not," she said.

He came closer, so close his eyes gleamed at her across the firelight. Though the moon was on the wane it was still full and bright. Washed in its light, he exerted a pull on her that was magical. Every fiber in her being yearned.

"No," she whispered. "I *must* not."

She banked her fire and walked into her tent where she lay in her sleeping bag with her hands balled into fists. Somewhere outside she could feel him, keeping his watch.

Chapter Four

October 31, 2001

Clarice came by earlier to bring me a bag of treats she'd made. She was in her usual Halloween getup—long black wig, green fright makeup, fake wart on her chin, tall pointy hat. I wish Michael could have seen her dress. She never wears the usual black. Makes my skin look sallow, she always says.

This year's garb was a red sequined tube with a tulle ruffle that flared around her calves.

"It makes you look like a mermaid," I said and she asked, "Yeah, but does it make me look sexy?"

She has a new boyfriend. Henry Somebody-or-Other. I can't keep up.

She told me, "He's coming trick-or-treating tonight, and I'm planning all kinds of tricks for him."

Leave it to Clarice.

She's outrageous. I used to be. Before Michael left. Having him to love made me more than I am, greater than the sum of my sagging parts.

I got to thinking about Halloweens past and I guess I started to cry because Clarice handed me a box of tissues and pulled up a chair as if she intended to stay all night. "Talk to me, Anne," she said.

That's all it took. "I was thinking about that time Michael made six dozen popcorn balls and not a single person showed up at our door."

"Why?"

"I think it stormed that year."

"Ninety-six. I remember it well. I was just back from Paris."

"Yes, that's when it was. Michael had just come back from filming in the Dolomites," I said.

"That movie with that great-looking Italian actress with the hips I'd kill for?"

"Yeah, that's the one. I guess that's why I figured I had to do something wild and crazy to get his attention."

"Shoot, Anne, you'd always had Michael's attention."

"Well, I know it, but still it never hurts to keep the excitement going.... I told Michael I was going to take a bath, and when he said he thought he'd join me, I told him, no, you stay here to answer the door just in case somebody comes."

"This is good already. I can just imagine what you were up to."

"Have I already told you this story? Stop me if I have."

"If you have I don't remember. See. All your secrets are safe with me, Anne."

"I know that. Anyhow, I stripped off my clothes, and

put on an old black trench coat of Michael's. Then I put on a long black wig and sneaked outside and rang the doorbell.''

Clarice was already laughing. "You didn't.''

"I did. Michael looked so cute when he opened the door, that expectant smile on his face and a basket of popcorn balls in his hands. 'Trick or treat!' I yelled, then I flung open the raincoat and stood there buck naked.''

By the time I got to that part I was laughing so hard I could barely talk.

"Don't leave me in suspense. What happened next?''

"I never expected to fool him, but I guess I did because he jumped backward and tripped over the umbrella stand. He hit it so hard he gashed his head, and I ended up taking him to the emergency room for stitches.''

Oh, it felt so good to laugh. I wish Clarice had stayed here all night, which was absolutely selfish of me. She has her own life, somebody waiting for her at home, somebody who will take her in his arms and tell her she's the most beautiful woman in the world, and then make love to her. All night if she wants to.

I can't bear to think about not having that again. I can't bear to think that Michael might never come back to me. What would I do?

I've been thinking a lot about that lately, about the possibility that he won't come back, that he'll stay in a coma and be forever remote, beyond my reach.

Yesterday I decided it was time to have a heart-to-heart talk with him. "Michael," I told him, "I've never wanted any man but you. The minute I saw you walking toward me in that bus terminal I knew you were the man I wanted to marry. And I've never been sorry, not one single day, even that time we got so mad at each other I left you and went to Mother's. I can't even remember what the fuss was all about. All I know is that you came after me the next morning and we spent all day in bed making up."

"Can you hear me, Michael? If you can, squeeze my hand."

I waited and waited, but nothing happened. And then I got scared that he might believe I was losing faith, and so I said, "That's all right, darling. You just take your time."

I lay down beside him and wrapped my arms around him and tried not to think about how frail he felt, how much weight he's lost since June. "It's all right, darling," I whispered. "I know you'll return to me. I'm right here, waiting for you."

Chapter Five

I wish I could talk to you, Anne. I wish I could tell you how much I love you and how hard I'm trying to return to you. Bear with me, my precious. Don't give up.

I'm coming back to you. I'm coming home.

Chapter Six

Hannah climbed with her cell phone and her backpack, expecting any moment to catch a glimpse of the wolfman, but there was no sign. The fact that she didn't see him made her uneasy for several reasons. Had misfortune befallen him or was he merely toying with her, setting her up for a nasty surprise?

She turned around to check the trail behind her once more, but all she saw were her own tracks in the newly fallen snow. Soon she'd have to leave. The snow would get deeper, making it nearly impossible for her to track either the wolves or the wolfman and dangerous for her to fly. Ice on the wings of a small plane could spell disaster.

She pulled off her right glove and punched in her editor's number.

"Jack, this is Hannah. What do you have for me?"

The connection was good, and she could hear him as plainly as if he were standing beside her in Denali.

"If what I think is true, we've hit the jackpot."

"What did you find out?"

"A small private plane went down in that area twenty years ago. Three people were in the plane—Conan Wolfe, a professor of history at Cornell, his wife Margaret who taught art at Cornell, and his son Hunter. Only two bodies were found."

Chills went down Hannah's spine. She knew the answer even before she asked the question.

"Who did the rescue party find?"

"Conan and Margaret. There was not a trace of the son."

"How old was he?"

"Nine...Hannah, we think the man you've found could be Hunter Wolfe."

"Impossible. A child that age couldn't have survived in this wilderness without help."

"From what you've said, we think he got it...from the wolves."

Possibilities swirled through her mind. Could it be true? There were the legends, of course. Romulus and Remus. There had been another case, documented, of a child having survived years in the wilds with no human companions.

"But Jack, couldn't this man simply be some old reclusive mountaineer who prefers the companionship of animals to that of man?"

"How old would you say he is, Hannah?"

"It's impossible to tell. All that wild hair and those skins he's wearing."

But the *body*...lean and fit. In spite of the skins she'd seen that for herself. She'd more than seen it, she'd felt it, and that was why she didn't say anything to Jack.

"That's why we want you to keep following him, Hannah. Get everything you can on film."

"The snows have started and are getting pretty heavy."

"Naturally we don't want you to take any unnecessary risks. Just do what you can, and we'll be there in a few days with a team."

"A team?"

"To capture him—"

The words sliced through Hannah and she barely heard the rest of what Jack was saying. After she'd hung up she stood on the mountain ledge looking out over the park and feeling like a traitor.

This magnificent creature she'd found, this wild man who stirred not only her imagination but her blood, was going to be hunted down and carried back to so-called civilization where he would be kept in confinement and studied as if he were nothing more than a guinea pig.

Of course that wasn't what Jack had said, but that was exactly what he had meant.

"What have I done?" she said.

More importantly what was she going to do?

All night Hannah wrestled with ethical and moral questions. In the wee hours of the morning, exhausted and almost unhinged, she somehow convinced herself that she was making a mountain out of a molehill, that Jack was too kind-hearted to do anything as barbaric as treat another human being like an animal. Clearly it would be in the wolfman's best interests to have an opportunity to reclaim his name and take his natural place in society.

She dressed then made coffee. The wolfman was nowhere in sight. If only she could see him once more. Then maybe she would know what to do.

The coffee was too strong. She managed to drink half a cup then tossed out the rest, disgusted with herself. She hated indecision.

A sound in a stand of nearby trees alerted her, and Hannah whirled around expecting to see the wolfman. Instead she saw the branch of a spruce tree bow under its heavy load and dump snow to the ground.

"Where are you?" she said. "Are you still out there?"

She stood in the middle of her camp clearing listening to the silence, then finally went inside to get her gear. She had a job to do.

Hannah didn't spot her quarry until mid morning. He was high above the campsite in a section of the park she had not explored. He stood on the ledge of a cliff in plain view, feet planted wide and hair blowing in the winds that howled around the mountain.

With the zoom lens it would make a perfect shot, but Hannah knew he would never give her the chance to get her camera up and focused. Instead she took a series of hip shots.

He watched her in perfect stillness, watched and waited. It occurred to Hannah that he had revealed himself to her deliberately. But why?

She cupped her hands around her mouth and shouted, "Hello, up there. What do you want?"

He didn't move. Had he heard? *Yes,* she would guess. The question was, how much did he understand?

"Come down. I want to talk to you."

He didn't respond, but neither did he vanish. Was she making progress with him?

"I won't hurt you." She held out both gloved hands. "See. I didn't bring my gun. No gun."

The sun that had been playing peekaboo all morning slipped from behind its cloud cover and bathed him in fierce light, made even more blinding by the reflected glare from the snow. Hannah reached for her sunglasses.

"Please come down. I'd like to talk to you."

She'd never seen another human being achieve such stillness. If it weren't for the wind through his hair and furs, she could have mistaken him for a lifelike carving.

"If you won't come down, I guess I'll have to come up." She shifted her backpack, sighing. She didn't relish the climb. Particularly not after a sleepless night.

As soon as she started to climb he began his own ascent, glancing over his shoulder every now and then to see that she followed. Hannah persevered for two hours.

"Thanks to Wheaties and Buns of Steel workouts," she muttered. She could barely see the wolfman in the distance, still climbing. "Hold on," she yelled. "What do you think I am? A mountain goat?"

He backtracked a few hundred feet, then sat on his haunches and stared down at her. Hannah glared right back.

"If you think I'm going to give up, you're mistaken. I never give up."

She pulled off her backpack and ate beef jerky while she surveyed her surroundings. She was at a much higher elevation than she'd expected...and in far more treacherous terrain.

Funny, she thought, how you can be in the midst of a thing and be unaware of the danger until you stop.

She'd climbed with her dad several times—once on McKinley. But never from this side of the mountain, never from this remote godforsaken section of Denali. If she went much higher she'd need equipment, which she didn't have. As a matter of fact, she probably shouldn't have climbed as far as she had without crampons, rope and an ice ax.

She finished her sparse lunch, then picked up her backpack. She'd allow no more than an hour to continue following the wolfman, then she'd have to head back to camp. To do otherwise would be foolhardy.

Besides, she'd gotten hardly any footage of him, so what was the point?

●

Fascination.

Well, there you had it. After years of solitary journeys into the heart of steamy jungles and wild canyons and treacherous mountains, she was going around the bend.

"Stop this," she said, talking to herself, and that was when she turned her ankle on a loose rock, lost her footing and began her terrifying fall down the side of the mountain.

Chapter Seven

The female lay at the bottom of the ravine. He crouched on the edge and peered down at her. She didn't move. He watched her for a long time, then finally made his way down to where she lay.

He smelled the blood before he got to her. Not much. Just a trickle coming from a small head wound. It matted her long black hair.

Crouched beside the fallen female, he studied her. Memories tugged at him and he was startled to discover moisture trickling from his eyes.

He reached out and touched her exposed skin. It was soft and still warm, and it filled him with a strange comfort.

There was something else, too—deep primitive urges that had driven him to lead her high into the mountains in search of safe territory where he might finally mate.

He bent down and sniffed her skin, then flicked his tongue over its smooth surface and sudden fire attacked his loins. He had chosen well. They would produce many offspring.

If she didn't die.

He licked her face again, then nipped at her soft lips and whined. She didn't move.

He sat back and studied the strange objects scattered around her. Her smell was on them. He pricked his skin on a sharp edge and a drop of his blood mingled with hers. She still lay with her eyes closed.

The pull of her was strong, and he curled up beside her and rested his head on her chest. The smell coming from her body reminded him of the meadow in summer. His loins stirred powerfully once more and he nipped at her neck trying to wake her.

A sound alerted him, and he looked up straight into the yellow eyes of a cougar. The great mountain cat was crouched and ready to spring on the fallen prey.

He leaped up, snarling, and the cat lifted its massive claws and spat at him. He could take the cat in a fight, and he wanted to, but instinct warned him to use the weapon he'd learned to make long before memory. He pulled an arrow out of his quiver, fitted it into the bow and aimed at the throat.

The cougar dropped, no longer a threat to the female.

He lifted his head and sniffed for further danger, then climbed out of the ravine and took watch on a ledge overlooking the fallen female.

Chapter Eight

November 4, 2001

The nursing home was in turmoil when I got here this morning. I heard the news first from the janitor because he was in the foyer on his hands and knees waxing the floor as if his life depended on it, and I nearly tripped over him coming in. I had my mouth open to apologize, but Bob beat me to it.

"Excuse me, Miz Westmoreland," he said, "I oughtn't been in your way." I told him it was my fault, that I hadn't been looking where I was going and he blurted out, "Well, everybody's in a uproar today 'cause Mr. Raines just up and quit."

According to Bob, the director couldn't take it any more, being around sick folks all the time. That's not what Vicky told me, though. When she brought in my breakfast tray she said, "I guess Mr. Raines is getting him a suntan right about now," and then she told me that he had run off to Tahiti with Nurse Schuster, of all people.

Any other time I would have wished them well because I believe in following your heart. I believe that people who ignore their hearts and follow reason consign themselves to a prosaic existence stripped of all wonder, all joy and all magic.

Right now, though, I can't think about the magic of true love: I can only think about what this change means for Michael. Sally Schuster was his primary care nurse, and Winslow Raines was in charge of everything that goes on here.

Who will make sure the glycerine swabs are lemon-scented? Who will see that the patients not only have their medicine, but their baths as well? Who will give the orders that clean hair is just as important as clean bed linens?

Mother came in to see Michael shortly after I got here.

"Anne, what are you doing, may I ask?"

Somehow that put me on the defensive, but then Mother frequently makes me feel as if I'm doing something wrong, even if I'm doing nothing more than pouring myself a glass of water.

"I'm gearing for battle," I told her.

Actually what I am doing is jotting notes so that when I meet the new director I'll know what to say, what to ask for. I learned that from Michael. He never went on a climb unprepared.

So, here's another mountain I have to climb. Because Michael is not here to climb it with me...and sometimes for me.

Four months ago I could have done this with one hand tied behind my back. Even two months ago while hope was still high. There was no problem too big, no situation too daunting.

Now I feel as if I'm drowning. Even the simple act of deciding what to have for supper takes too much effort.

Last night I stood in front of the refrigerator for ten minutes, the sight of lettuce as foreign to me as if I had landed from Mars.

I want somebody to decide for me. I want Michael.

Well, there's the phone ringing. I don't feel like talking. Even a simple conversation seems too much effort.

But what if it's one of the children? Daniel and Skylar to talk about Thanksgiving plans, or Emily and Jake just back from their honeymoon? What if it's Hannah?

Lord, I hope it's Hannah. I haven't heard from her in days, and I know it's about time for her to be coming home.

Chapter Nine

Hannah regained consciousness slowly, disoriented at first, then stunned by the magnitude of her dilemma. She was at the bottom of a deep ravine, surrounded by walls so sheer she had no hope of climbing out. Even if she could climb.

She assessed the damage. There was blood in her hair, but the wound on her scalp felt superficial. Her body ached, but everything seemed to be in working order except her left ankle. It hurt to move, and she could feel the swelling already pressing against her boot.

It was amazing that she'd survived such a fall with so little damage. She had her thick winter clothing to thank plus the scrub brush that had broken her long plunge.

She remembered slipping over the edge, remembered her surprise, then her outrage. At first she'd thought, *I can't believe this,* then as she'd tumbled from bush to bush, *Ok, this is not so bad. I'm going to be all right.*

And then there was that last rude shock. She'd landed on her wings. That's what her daddy used to call her shoulder blades. As she scooted and came to a stop her left foot had ricocheted against a rock. Pain shot through her, but still she was thinking, *It's over,* when her neck whiplashed and her head bashed against a rock.

Then silence. How long had she been knocked out?

Her watch crystal was broken but the dial still glowed. Six o'clock.

A long ululant cry filled the night. She could make out the shape towering above her, the wolfman with his head lifted toward the pale sliver of moon.

"Hello, up there," she yelled. "Is there a way out of here?"

No answer. What had she expected? She was on her own.

Hannah felt around in the dark for her supplies. Parts of her camera were scattered across the rock. Her backpack had burst open and its contents spilled everywhere. She found one piece of jerky and started to eat it then reconsidered. That was all that stood between her and starvation. She'd ration it while she tried to figure out what to do.

Where was her cell phone? Her water?

She crawled in ever-widening circles trying to locate them, and finally gave up. She had no idea what was out there in the dark.

Huddled against the shelter of a rock she rolled herself into a tight ball for warmth. Tomorrow she'd find the rest of her things. Tomorrow she'd find a way out of here.

With her head pillowed against her backpack she gazed at the top of the cliff. The wolfman was still keeping watch. Somehow that comforted her.

* * *

In the morning she found the dead cougar. At first she thought another animal had killed him, then she saw the single jagged neck wound.

"You did this?"

She glanced at her protector. He had not moved from his spot atop the cliff, and in the daylight she could see why. It commanded a view of the entire area.

She wondered if he had slept. Probably not. He had the look of someone who was keeping guard, a tense, ready-for-action look. Hannah wished she had her camera.

She covered her mouth to stifle a giggle. Hysteria wouldn't do. She had to stay calm.

"Did you kill the cougar to protect me?" she yelled.

This time she got a response. He moved around the edge of the cliff so he could position himself right above her.

"Did you make the shot from up there or did you come down here?"

She searched the rock face for footholds. Her head hurt, her ankle throbbed and her throat was parched. There would be no relief. She could see the bright red rim of her thermos on an outcropping of rock near the top of the cliff, with what appeared to be her cell phone lying nearby.

"This does not look good," she said, and then she began a systematic search for a way out of the ravine.

Darkness dropped like a curtain, and Hannah sank onto a small boulder, exhausted and weak. Her hands were bloody from failed attempts at climbing. She'd had only one small bite of jerky all day and no water. There was no way she could survive without water.

The wolfman was still up there watching her. He'd watched all day, adjusting his position as she'd roamed looking for escape.

She had made no further attempts to talk to him. What

was the use? He couldn't understand her and she had to conserve her strength.

Maybe she'd think of something tomorrow. She crawled into her bed of rocks and tumbled into the blessed oblivion of sleep.

Someone was calling her name. "Hannah...Hannah. Can you hear me?"

"I hear you. Daddy? Daddy, is that you?"

"Yes," he said, and suddenly Michael was there, not the fading father she'd last seen lying in a narrow white bed but a younger, robust version of him, the black-haired, green-eyed laughing man she remembered from childhood.

"How did you find me, Daddy?"

"You called me."

"I want to go home now, but I've lost the way."

"You'll find a way. Don't give up, Hannah. Don't give up."

She wanted to ask him questions. She wanted to say, How will I find a way? but Michael was fading and in his place was the shadow of a tall man backlit by the moon, a man with long flowing hair that glinted silver under the stars.

Hannah woke up crying. High above her the wolfman looked like something carved from the mountain.

"Help me," she called, knowing that soon her voice would be too weak to carry. "Help me."

There was no movement from above, no sound. "Please, please help me." Still he didn't move.

She lay back in her rocky bed, spent.

Don't give up.

"Daddy," she called, but she knew he'd only been a dream. There was no one to help Hannah except a man who had lived among wolves so long she didn't know whether he had any language left or any capacity for human feeling.

Suddenly inspiration seized her, and she yelled at the top of her voice.

"Hunter Wolfe!"

He dropped into a crouch and leaned far over the edge of the cliff to peer down at her. Hannah couldn't believe it.

Did he recognize his name? Did it trigger some memory?

She dragged herself into a sitting position and lifted her arms toward him.

"Hunter Wolfe, help me. Help me!"

He leaped into the air and for a heady moment she thought he was flying. Then she saw the rope, and as she watched in amazement the man she'd called Hunter Wolfe descended into the ravine.

Chapter Ten

November 4, 2001

I can't bear to look at Michael. I can't bear to talk to him for fear I'll let everything I'm feeling slip out, and oh, that would be too horrible. I love him. He's my life, my heart, my soul. I want him to know that, to believe it, and yet...

Well, I might as well write it all down so I don't forget, so I don't slip up and let it happen again. Here's what happened: I spent the night at Belle Rose so I would feel fresh this morning when I cornered the Bear (Clarice's term, not mine). The new director here is Larry Baird. "He looks just like a great big old cuddly teddy bear," Clarice told me after she saw him in the hall, and I told her, I don't care what he looks like, I'm not putting up with sloppy care from the new nurse. She didn't even check Michael's pressure points, and besides that she didn't even talk to him.

Say something to him, I told her, Let him know who you are and that you care, and she said, "I have thirty other patients. I don't have time to spend talking to one."

Cold, that's what she is. And bordering on incompetent. I will not sit back and let my husband get bedsores. Nor will I see him treated like a piece of meat.

So this morning I put on the blue sweater Michael likes and marched into the director's office with my list of complaints. Ready to take on a passle of wild cats on behalf of my beloved.

After I'd introduced myself I said, "Mr. Baird, the new nurse is not doing her job and I want the situation rectified."

"What seems to be the problem?"

He pulled off his glasses, and right out of the blue I noticed they were the wire-rimmed kind that made him look sexy. I had no business at all noticing such a thing, so I jerked my list out of my purse and started shaking so bad he hurried over and took my hands and said, "There, there, Mrs. Westmoreland. Your husband has been here a long time, and I know how hard that is for you."

Well, you can imagine what all that sympathy did to me. All of a sudden I was bawling like a calf in a hailstorm and this new director was hugging me and I was sobbing all over his shirt and it felt so good to be held I didn't want him to let go.

As a matter of fact, he didn't. He held onto me saying things like, "You go ahead and cry, Take your time, I'm not going anywhere."

Oh, it has been so long and it felt so good...

I can't remember how long I stood there with his arms around me, but I can remember what I was thinking. I was thinking, If Michael doesn't come back, another man just might be possible.

Not that he could ever take Michael's place, or even come close. Not that anyone else would ever, ever make me feel the magic. There is only one true soul mate, and Michael is mine. I know that.

I knew it this morning when I stood in that office like a ninny and let this strange man put his hands all over me.

Well, not all over me. Not really. He never called me anything except Mrs. Westmoreland. He never did a thing except offer a friendly shoulder to cry on.

I was the one making more out of it than a simple gesture of kindness. I was the emotional one. I was thinking, The door is closed and we're alone and nobody has to know. Any minute he's going to kiss me and I'm going to kiss him back, and who knows where that will lead?

For one awful moment I wanted that to happen. I wanted to be swept away by a kiss. I wanted to be swamped with passion. I actually imagined rolling around on the carpet with a man who called me Mrs. Westmoreland.

I don't know who I am anymore. I can't seem to hold onto myself as Anne Westmoreland whose husband adores her. I can't picture myself as Anne Westmoreland, mother of three adult children and mother-in-law to two fine people. Any day now I could be a grandmother, and yet I can't see myself that way, either.

All of a sudden I'm this new woman seeing the possibilities for sex behind every closed door and feeling my sap rise and rise and rise...with nowhere to go.

I guess I ought to be ashamed, but that's the odd thing: I'm not. Don't get me wrong. I still feel as if I've betrayed my husband on some level, and yet on some primitive level I feel this secret glee. I'm alive, I want to shout. There's still a spark in me that won't be squelched, no matter what.

Maybe I will tell Michael, after all. Maybe he needs to know that I didn't dry up and blow away simply because he left. Do I hurt? *Yes.* Loss is a monster that eats away at me every day. But I'm still here. I'm still *me.*

Maybe that's what I needed to discover this morning in Director Baird's office, that no matter what happens there's a spark inside me that refuses to be extinguished. I will survive. I know this now.

No, not merely survive. I will triumph.

Chapter Eleven

Hannah was awestruck. Hunter Wolfe stood not two feet from her, and every coherent thought she had flew out of her head. She was actually up close with the wolfman, that's all she could think. She tried to take in everything at once, but couldn't get past his eyes. They mesmerized her, those startling silver lasers. They burned through her with an intensity that made her shiver. And once she started she couldn't seem to stop.

She wrapped her arms around herself and spoke through chattering teeth, "Get me out of here." He stood there staring at her. "Please."

That seemed to be the magic word, for suddenly he scooped her up, and then, holding her as if she weighed no more than a kitten, he leaped toward the rope that dangled from the cliff.

Dizziness swamped Hannah...and sensation. Cocooned in fur she felt both safe and terrified. His arms were bands of steel, his face chiseled stone, his hair a golden thicket that blew into her face as they swung upward.

Out of the corner of her eye she spotted her thermos and her cell phone.

"Wait, please. I need to get that." He hesitated and she reached out and snatched up her prized possessions. At last, water. She uncapped the bottle and swigged only enough to sooth her parched throat while he watched her.

There was both curiosity and intelligence in his eyes. "Thank you," she whispered, and then they were airborne again, swinging high above the ravine that had almost claimed her life.

It would have if Hunter Wolfe hadn't rescued her. When they reached the top, he placed her gently on a rock, then stood sentinel as if he'd been given a commission from some unknown source.

The bearskins he wore had been fashioned into crude pants and tunic and did nothing to hide the fact that he was wondrously made...and exuberantly male. Hannah felt the heat from the roots of her hair all the way down to her toes.

In a matter of moments she'd changed from a woman about to die at the bottom of a ravine to a woman ignited by sexual fires that stole reason. This was no animal standing before her but a man, a man who was driving her crazy.

She had to do something, anything.

"Thank you," she said. "You saved my life."

And then she touched him. He didn't flinch, didn't move, and she wound her battered hand around his and held on.

"If you hadn't come for me, I would have died at the bottom of that ravine."

He glanced at her hand, and then slowly his fingers closed around hers. His hands were powerful, like the rest of him. She'd never been in the presence of a man who exuded such power, such male energy. It was like standing in front of a blazing furnace.

She wanted to lean on him. She wanted to feel his arms around her once more. She wanted to bury her face in the skins he wore and cry until there were no more tears.

Hannah had never felt this way in her life. She could blame fatigue and exposure for her feelings, but she was too smart. There was something else at work here, something she didn't dare analyze.

All she knew was that she could not let Jack take this man off the mountain and put him in a cage, for that's what tight confinement would be to him. Instinctively she knew that something wonderful and magical, some spark deep inside him would die. And she wasn't about to let that happen.

When she stood up, her face was only inches from his. He didn't move, but she stepped back so fast she would have fallen if he hadn't caught her. And held on. Oh, he held on, and it felt so good Hannah felt like swooning.

"You have to come with me," she said. "Come with me. Back to my camp. Come, Hunter Wolfe. Please, come."

He picked her up and started down the mountain. Did he understand or did he merely sense that she needed rest in her own surroundings, much like a wounded she-wolf returning to her den?

Why question fate? With the moon and the stars lighting their path, Hannah curled her hand into his fur tunic and leaned her head against his chest, just to rest, just for a moment.

The female was sleeping. That was good. Sleep would heal.

He moved swiftly through the night. Soon the snows

would fall again, and he wanted to get her back into her den before they came.

Strange feelings coursed through him. What was that name she called him? It echoed in his mind and stirred long-buried memories: fire, so much fire, and screams that had haunted him for years.

He put them out of his mind so he could focus on the task at hand. He would have taken her to his cave, but her den was closer. He crawled inside with her, put her in her nest then lay down beside her. Her body was soft and sweet-smelling. It seemed natural to hold on.

Hannah woke with a start and found herself staring straight into the eyes of her rescuer. Furthermore, he was wrapped so closely around her, she couldn't have moved if she'd wanted to.

And she definitely didn't want to. They stared at each other with frank curiosity. And something else, too. A sexual awareness that was almost palpable. He was fully aroused and not at all embarrassed by the fact, and she was having fantasies that made her skin burn.

She touched his face. "Who are you?" she whispered. "Are you Hunter Wolfe? Are you the little boy lost in the wilderness, all grown up?"

He didn't blink, didn't move. Only his eyes seemed alive. They studied her with an intensity that made her shiver.

She could not let Jack take this man. She *would* not.

"They're going to send men here to capture you. Do you understand anything I'm saying? They're going to keep you in a facility that will be nothing more than a cage to you."

The thought of Hunter Wolfe in confinement brought tears to her eyes, but Hannah didn't care. All that mattered now was getting her rescuer to safety.

As she leaned over him, her hair and her tears fell on his face.

"I can't let them take you. Come with me. You must come with me."

Chapter Twelve

November 6, 2001

The most amazing thing has happened. I still can't believe it. Another secret I have to keep from Michael. (I didn't tell him, after all, about Larry Baird. Just in case he's been holding on until I found somebody else; just in case he would say to himself, Hmmm, all right, Anne is going to be okay now, she has somebody else to take care of her, so I can fall into this deep dark sleep and not bother about trying to find my way home.)

That's not true, of course. I don't know what happened yesterday, but it will never happen again. I saw Larry Baird when I got here this morning, and he was nothing to me except a slightly paunchy guy with a bad haircut. Nothing at all. Of course, I stopped to chat when he said, "Good morning." Anything less would have been impolite, as Mother has so often told me, but

I can say in all honesty that the thought of him touching me made my skin crawl. And not in a good way.

Anyhow, back to this big secret: Hannah called me. From Denali. She said, "Mom, go out and buy some men's shirts, large, and some pants, probably 34 waist and inseam, and a pair of men's jogging shoes, size ll. No, better make that l2. And buy food, too. Lots of red meat and fish."

I asked her, What's going on? and expected her to say something like, I'm bringing home an indigent Alaskan, but of course, with Hannah nothing is ever that simple. When she told me about Hunter Wolfe, I naturally asked the question on any mother's mind. "Is he dangerous?" I said.

She didn't answer me, not directly anyhow. She said, "I have to bring him home, Mom. I have to save him because he saved me."

When she told me how she fell into that ravine, and how he got her out I relived those awful days of Michael's accident. I nearly lost two of them, was all I could think.

Are you all right? was what I asked her first, and she told me yes, her cuts were superficial and she'd tended them, and then I said, "If this man really is Hunter Wolfe, and if he's been living in the wilderness for twenty years without human contact, how did you ever convince him to fly home with you?"

"I don't know. I used gestures, pantomime, everything I could think of, but I think it was my tears that did the trick."

Hannah, in tears! That's unbelievable. Nothing short of a miracle. It occurs to me that something more is going on here than a simple rescue.

Yesterday I bought the clothes she asked for then

drove to her place on the river. It's so peaceful up there I felt like staying. I told her I'd get Clarice to stay with Michael and I would be there when she arrived with this wild man, but she told me, No, Mom, I have to do this by myself. Besides, she told me, the fewer people who know, the safer he will be.

"How are you going to handle Jack?" I asked, and she said, "I called and told him the wolfman fell into a ravine and died. When he asked how I could be certain, I told him blood was everywhere, that I went back the next day to be sure and wild animals had already ravaged the body."

"Did he believe you?"

"He has no cause to think otherwise."

"I don't want you to jeopardize everything you've worked for."

"I won't. Besides, I'm freelance, Mom. Jack's not the only game in town."

I was worried about the flight, too, because she said the snows have already started and I thought about her flying that light plane with ice on the wings.

Be careful, I told her, and she promised she would, though I know she won't. Caution is not in Hannah's nature.

Chapter Thirteen

It was one thing to be in the same park as Hunter Wolfe, and quite another to be confined in the cockpit of a twin-engine plane. He sat in the passenger seat as forbidding as a strange monolith, his arsenal of weapons resting across his lap. There was the rope he'd used to rescue her—vines twisted together in an ingenious way—a lethal-looking handmade knife, his bow and the bearskin quiver filled with handmade arrows, their tips razor-sharp. She knew this because she'd already pricked her finger trying to help him get in the plane.

When he'd seen the blood, he'd bellowed in outrage, then lifted her off her feet and set her aside while he climbed aboard. She got in on the other side, wondering how he'd react when she tried to buckle him in.

"Buckle up," she said, and when she fastened her own buckles he watched her, then did the same. No fumbling, no hesitation.

There was no doubt about it: this man was extremely intelligent. She planned to take a show-and-tell approach with him. Though he hadn't tried to utter a word, he listened intently to everything she said. Maybe he understood more than she'd thought.

"I'm going to start the engine now. It will be very noisy. I know you crashed in a small plane, but I'm a very good pilot. Don't be afraid."

She needn't have worried. He watched every move she made, and when the engine roared to life he didn't even blink. That shouldn't have surprised her. He'd lived on the edge for twenty years where every act was a matter of survival, even getting his food.

"This is going to be a long trip, so just settle back and relax."

She wished he wouldn't stare at her that way. He made her hot all over just by looking at her. Take this morning, for instance...

When she'd wakened up with him wrapped around her and looking at her as if he planned to have her for breakfast, she'd nearly joined the wild herself. If he'd touched her she would have done anything he wanted. *Anything*.

So what in the world was she going to do with him in her house?

Educate him. Help him reclaim his birthright.

Oh, yeah?

Hannah was glad her brother wasn't here. Daniel would see through her in a minute.

"Let me tell you about the place where we're going. I live on five hundred acres on the Mississippi River, so you shouldn't feel caged in. There's plenty of room for you to roam."

He never took his eyes off her. How much did he understand?

"My land used to be part of a plantation, but everything burned in the War Between the States except a silo. It's handmade slate, really quite beautiful. I used to think about converting it into a place to live, but it was one of those things I never got around to. My cottage is small, but since I travel a lot, size doesn't seem to matter."

She had a sudden vision of herself in close quarters with Hunter. Night and day. For how long? How long would it take to educate him? To civilize him?

It was a pity she couldn't consult experts, but hers had to be a solo mission. She gave a rueful chuckle. Weren't they always? She was too stubborn to take orders and too irascible for polite company.

As she flew south she pointed out the different states and kept up a running commentary that was both geography and history lesson. He listened and looked, but nothing moved him from his cocoon of silence.

More than once Hannah wondered what she had gotten into and why, but she wasn't about to back down. Once she committed to a project, she would go through hell and high water in order to see it through to the end.

What can the end be for Hunter Wolfe?

She firmly shoved the question from her mind. Why borrow trouble? She'd never been one to worry over what might be. Her philosophy was to grab life by the throat and live to the fullest every moment of every day. When she came to the end of her life she didn't want to regret the things she hadn't done. Sure, she'd probably miss a few things along the way, but it wouldn't be from cowardice or lack of trying.

They arrived home at sunset. Hannah banked the plane so they appeared to be floating on a golden path that led straight to the Mississippi River. She always tried to time her trips so she would be flying into the setting sun, and the sight never failed to take her breath away.

"That's my home down there. Beautiful, isn't it? I know Denali is spectacular, but no matter where I travel I'm always glad to get home. I guess it's true what they say, There's no place like home."

She turned to smile at her passenger. "Dorothy, *Wizard of Oz.* I'll have to introduce you to the old books and movies. I love them."

She had a sudden vision of her parents sitting side by side on the sofa holding hands and laughing at old Laurel and Hardy movies. She'd call her mother as soon as she got Hunter settled in.

As she taxied to a stop, Hannah thanked her lucky stars that she had a private airstrip. There was no one to gawk as Hunter emerged from the plane like some primitive war god, complete with ancient weapons.

Typically, the capricious Mississippi weather fooled her. She hadn't expected cold weather—that happened only sporadically from October through December with the real "cold spells," as her grandmother called them, holding off until January and February—but she had expected something cooler than the heat that wafted up from the tarmac. It felt like being in a steam bath.

"You'll want to get out of that bearskin. I have some clothes for you inside."

He followed her through the front door, but she'd never seen a more cautious entry. He was as tense and suspicious as if he expected something wild to attack him from every quarter.

The clothes were lying on the sofa. "Good, my mom came through for us."

She walked over and picked them up. Now what was she going to do? Would he remember?

"These are your clothes." He didn't move, didn't respond. "You take off your skins...." She took off her own flight jacket to demonstrate, then pointed to him. "Take off clothes. See."

Lord, she might as well have said, Me Jane, you Tarzan.

All of a sudden his weapons clattered to the floor and he started stripping off bearskin.

"No...wait...Not here." His boots flew to one corner of the room, his tunic to the other. "No...wait a minute..."

God, his chest was gorgeous. Broad, muscular, all that great chest hair tipped golden from the sun.

His hands were on his pants. "No...not here," she said, but she didn't sound convincing, even to herself. And when his pants fell to the floor and he stood before her gorgeously, gloriously naked, every coherent thought flew from her head.

"Oh my..."

Hannah did what any sane woman would do: she feasted her eyes. There was no telling what else she might have done if he hadn't walked out the door. Stark naked.

"Thank God, I don't have neighbors," she muttered to herself as she followed him. What else was there to do? She hadn't brought him all the way from Alaska to lose him on the first day home.

He was up ahead, setting a fast pace. "Wait," she yelled. He didn't slow down. "If you think you can get away from me, you'd better think again."

She'd grown up racing her brother along the bluffs of the Mississippi. She wasn't about to let a wolfman from Alaska beat her.

She started running, gritting her teeth against the pain that shot through her ankle. It took her ten minutes to catch up to him.

"See, I warned you. You can't get away from me."

He didn't slow down, but he did turn and smile at her. Hannah felt as if she'd won a journalism award.

"I would have caught you sooner if it hadn't been for this bum ankle."

He was headed to the river. It was just ahead, its waters still tinted pink and gold from the sun. What was he planning to do? Jump in and try to swim home?

She wasn't long finding out. One minute he was on the bluff, and the next he was flying through the air. Hannah raced to the edge in time to see him slice through the water. In a natural, unstudied way he had executed a dive that would be the envy of Olympic contenders.

She couldn't dive in after him. The bluff was too high. She'd break her neck...or worse...crash two feet short of the water and break every bone in her body.

She could make her way down the bluff, but it was deeply wooded, and she'd lose sight of him before she reached the bottom. Besides, there was her ankle. There was nothing to do but wait and see what was going to happen.

The water closed around him, and for a moment he was back in the icy waters of his home with nothing more to think about than where his next meal would come from. He dived deep, and when he came up he saw the female on the bluff.

Hannah, she called herself. *Hannah.* Her name.

Hunter. His name.

Confusion crashed around him once more, and no matter how far out he swam, it followed. There was so much to learn, so much to understand.

In addition, there were the urgent stirrings of his loins. Every time he looked at Hannah.

He longed for his wilderness. Life was elemental there. He ate, he slept. And soon he would mate.

It was time.

He glanced upward, and the pull of her was stronger than the moon. Hunter stepped from the water and began to climb.

Oh, God, what am I going to do with this gorgeous naked man? This gorgeous naked, wet man?

"I'll bet you're hungry," she said. His face said, Yes, and his eyes swept over her as if he meant to have her for the meal.

Hannah tried to keep her eyes focused on his face. "There's food in the house. Follow me."

Call her coward, but she turned from him and practically ran toward her cottage. Thankfully, she saw that he followed.

The first thing she was going to do when she got back was see if she couldn't get him to put on some clothes.

Chapter Fourteen

November 6, 2001

I've become a bona fide liar.

Oh, I didn't mean to. It just happened. First there was that incident with Larry Baird, which I kept from Michael, and now there's Hannah. She called a little while ago, and wouldn't you know, Clarice was here in the house. Belle Rose. I couldn't bear to stay at the nursing home tonight. I don't know why.

Well, yes, I do. I can't bear to lie beside Michael and not have him touch me. I can't stand to lie there hoping and hoping while nothing ever happens.

Anyhow, Clarice breezed in and plopped a chicken casserole on the kitchen table.

"I've brought our supper," she said, "and afterward we'll watch X-rated movies."

"I don't have any X-rated movies," I said, and she pulled two out of a sack and said, "Now you do."

She's such a good friend, such good company. Lord, I remember how we laughed the last time she decided it would do us both good to watch an X-rated movie. "See something we can drool over," was the way she put it. It was right after Michael got over that bout of pneumonia, I think.

Anyhow, I set the table with those china plates I love, the ones Michael brought from Japan, and we were both eating our second helping when Hannah called.

"Mother," she said, and I knew right away something was wrong because my children never call me Mother unless they're upset.

"What's wrong, Hannah?"

"I had dinner with a naked man...fish that he ate raw, mind you...and then I tried for an hour to convince him to put on his clothes...I guess I'll have to do it for him...and now he's holed up in his bedroom with the door shut and I'm scared to go in there and scared not to because I just don't know what he's going to do next. God, what am I going to do?"

Clarice was all ears, and besides, how could I advise my daughter when I don't have the faintest idea how to deal with any situation these days, let alone one as bizarre as she described?

"Well, Hannah, I guess you'll just have to make the best of things."

"That's it! That's all you can say?"

"Yes. Clarice and I are going to watch a movie."

"I see. You can't talk because Clarice is there."

"That's right."

I felt like such a fraud, blaming Clarice. But that was easier than telling the truth: I'm falling apart piece by piece and nobody notices. Not even Clarice. Not really.

If she did she'd be hauling shrinks through the door...in addition to X-rated movies.

That's one of the reasons I love Clarice. She believes in the curative powers of laughter.

"I'll call you tomorrow," I told my daughter, and after Hannah hung up, Clarice and I spent the next three hours watching things that made us laugh so hard we cried.

I needed that.

Chapter Fifteen

Hannah lay in bed with her eyes wide open. How could she sleep when she didn't know what Hunter would do next? She was so frustrated she wanted to hit something, so she punched her pillow. Hard. Then she struck it again.

What if Hunter decided to leave and find his way back to the wilderness? There was no way she could stop him.

So far she hadn't done a very good job of leading him gently into society. Maybe he would have been better off if she'd simply told her big fat lie to Jack, then left Hunter in the wilderness. Certainly *she* would have been better off.

"Hind sight is twenty-twenty," she muttered as she pummeled her pillow once more.

A sound caught her attention. The guest bedroom door opening.

"Thank goodness for squeaky hinges," she thought as she started to leap out of bed, then thought better of it.

Perhaps he was just going to the bathroom. If she followed wouldn't she look foolish?

Not that she cared. In general Hannah didn't give a rat's behind what people thought of her as long as she thought well of herself.

Her father had taught her about self-esteem. And her mother.

Lord, that was another thing. If she'd left Hunter in the wilderness where she'd found him, if she'd never made that phone call to Jack in the first place, she would be at Belle Rose now helping her mom and seeing about her dad.

She didn't hear footfalls, but then what had she expected? Here was a man who had spent twenty years sneaking up on caribou. He would know how to walk without sounding like a St. Patrick's Day parade.

Why didn't she hear his bedroom door again? How long did it take a man in the bathroom at night? She wouldn't know, never having observed her father and her brother that closely. And she'd had neither the time nor the inclination to find out otherwise.

Men were just plain too much trouble. Besides, they cramped her lifestyle and weighed her down with expectations which she would never in a million years meet. Nor would she want to. She'd learned that the hard way her senior year in college when she and George Crayton III, had shared a few meals and a less-than-satisfying romp or two.

What was taking Hunter so long?

She listened for a while, then flung back the covers and raced toward the front door, groaning ''What was I thinking?''

Hunter Wolfe didn't know about toilets, and how in the world was she ever going to show him short of demonstrating? Just another small detail she hadn't thought of before she'd snatched him out of the wilderness.

He was obviously outside somewhere, and she was going to find him…no matter what he was up to.

She banged through her front door and raced around her cottage, but he was nowhere to be found.

"Hunter, Hunter Wolfe! Where are you?"

Her only answer was the call of an owl deep in the woods. What had she expected?

"Think, think…"

If she had been plucked from the wilderness and set down in unfamiliar territory, where would she go?

To the river. She was off and running, never mind that her left ankle felt as if hot pins were being jabbed into it. Tomorrow she had to do something about that. There was an Ace bandage somewhere in her cottage, left over from a sprained ankle she'd got when she was covering a story in the Andes two years ago.

In the distance she saw the river, pale and shining in the moonlight. Hannah rounded a copse of oak trees, and there he was, Hunter Wolfe with his face turned toward the water.

He whirled around when he heard her, and all of a sudden she was vividly aware of her own body—tingling and hot—much, much too hot. In spite of the chill in the night air and the fact that she was wearing only an oversized white sleep shirt with a slogan that read, Give In To Your Animal Instincts…Save the Mountain Gorilla, in big red letters right across her breasts. Her traitorous breasts that were suddenly tight and turgid and not at all shy about advertising her condition.

Just as he was advertising his…

She couldn't move, couldn't think.

"Hunter," she whispered, and he took a step toward her.

"Let's go back…" His eyes burned through her and words became redundant.

He took another step, then another, and Hannah drew a deep breath.

They were inevitable.

He touched her hair, her cheek, her lips, and the gentleness was so unexpected she felt the sting of tears. They ran down her face and into the corners of her mouth. She was drowning in tears…and in the molten silver of his eyes.

He bent down and nuzzled the side of her neck. Shivers shook her from head to toe. Her bones melted, and suddenly her knees wouldn't hold her.

He caught her as she started down, his movements swift and sure as he arranged her…hands and knees on the forest floor, fragrant with the scent of pine.

She whispered his name as he slid her nightshirt out of the way, then yes, yes, yes as he thrust deep inside. Her cries blended with his, echoing through the night woods in a sound both primitive and strangely sensual.

The moon hung low over the river, the waters whispered her name and the trees bent down to listen. Hannah was one with them, one with every good and perfect creation of nature.

She was no longer a woman on her knees in the forest with the wolfman driving into her with a force that would have knocked her to the ground if he hadn't braced her. She was moon and comet and stars. She was earth and sky and water. She was wisdom and knowledge and sensation. So much sensation she couldn't contain it.

Her pleasure cries rang through the forest. He was insatiable, primitive and wild…and so erotic she convulsed time after time. Every inch of her body was sensitized. Even her scalp. She was aware of the roots of her hair and each individual pore in her skin, of the coursing of her blood and the racing of her heart.

Each breath she took intensified the thrill, and from a distance she heard herself saying, Please, please, please, then Oh, *Yes!* as his warmth flooded her. Her own explosions shook her so hard she would have fallen if he hadn't held on, held on tight.

When he broke away she whimpered, ''No, please,'' and suddenly he wrapped himself around her, and she lay in the pine needles curled tightly against him.

The stars had never looked so bright.

He listened to the sound of the female's even breathing.

Hannah. Her name whispered through him, then roared, and with it all the things he'd learned since leaving his wilderness and the company of his brothers, the wolves.

The plane, the house, the furniture, the food…all of it was foreign to him and yet familiar in a disturbing way. Memories assaulted him, and with them the words. They were coming back. Rapidly. Hannah had opened a storehouse and unearthed the language that had been deeply buried.

His head swam with the enormity of what was happening. It was too much. Too much excitement, too much pain.

The only surcease he had was in her. His loins stirred once more and he sought the sweet musky scent rising from her. When he tasted her, she was instantly alert.

''Hunter?'' There was a softness in her when she touched his face, and he longed to say her name. Longed to but dared not. Not yet.

He positioned her then drove into her so hard she rocked forward. The power his need had over him frightened him. With Hannah he was both master and slave, the hunter and the hunted.

This was no mere mating. Instinctively he knew it was more. He had no name for what it was, only the certainty that it might change him forever.

The hot, hard thrills overtook her once more, and she said to herself, I won't think about what I'm doing, I can't.

Then she surrendered, and passion unlike any she'd ever known swallowed her.

"This," she whispered, as he drove into her, strong and bold and powerful. "Yes, yes...this..."

The truth branded her mind and settled into her bones.

She wouldn't think about yesterday or tomorrow. She would hold the moment. Only the moment.

For as long as it lasted.

Chapter Sixteen

It lasted until dawn.

Afterward, Hannah lay curled against him knowing she had to get up and leave this enchanted place, but not wanting to. Wouldn't it be great if she could keep him on her five hundred acres as a playmate? They could run around without their clothes on until the weather drove them inside. She'd be his love slave until she had to go off on assignment to earn their keep, and when she came home he'd be waiting.

That kind of thinking was such a departure for her, she laughed aloud. Hunter raised on his elbows to study her, his expressive eyes asking the questions he could not. Or would not. Which was it?

"I was just daydreaming," she said. "They were silly dreams, really. Impossible. Not at all practical."

He smiled then, and she would swear she knew what he was thinking. *No dream is silly.* That's what she heard.

Once she'd read that when two people have been intimate in a way that touches the soul, they can sometimes read each other's thoughts and send telepathic messages.

Hunter leaned down and nipped at her neck. She'd seen wolves doing that in the wild. It was part of their courtship ritual, and not confined to the brief period before they mated. Wolves often demonstrated their affection in playful moments.

She cupped his face. "What are you thinking right now? I wish I knew." He had the most expressive eyes she'd ever seen, and he was studying her with an intensity that made her hot. Again.

Lord, that was getting to be a constant state with her. Wouldn't Emily laugh if she knew.

"For whatever this is worth, that was the most phenomenal sex I've ever had. Absolutely over the moon. Of course I understand this is only physical, so please don't think I'm like those women who read love into every encounter.

"You don't know what I'm talking about, do you? And you certainly don't know any other women."

The idea of being his first pleased her more than it should have, particularly since their wild mating was nothing more than a force of nature. Nothing could ever come of it. A relationship with the wolfman was out of the question. Impossible.

"If we keep this up..." He smiled and she flushed. "...and I expect we will since it's...natural." His smile got wider. Lord, what if he understood every word she was saying? "There are some things I can teach you. Not that you're not already phenomenal."

Almost a god.

Lord, she had to get a hold of herself.

Here she was sitting in the middle of the woods on a

chilly November morning wearing nothing but a nightshirt twisted up around her waist...and all she could think about was their next erotic encounter.

"I think we should go back. I don't know about you, but I'm hungry and I could use a bath. Anyhow, we need to get started with your education."

Heat flooded her face once more. What they'd done in the woods was certainly educational. But who was the teacher and who the pupil?

Look on the bright side, she told herself. There was no longer any need to be shy about showing him the wonders of modern plumbing.

"Hannah, are you all right?"

Her mother couldn't have called at a worse time because they'd both had baths—together—and neither of them had on a stitch and Hunter was looking at her in that certain way that she already understood.

"I'm fine, Mom."

"Well, I didn't know. After last night...look, darling, I'm sorry I couldn't be of more help, but Clarice was there and quite frankly I didn't know what to tell you. I still don't."

Hunter was stalking her now. That was the only way she could put it. Never mind that she was on the telephone. He had the look of a man who wasn't going to let a little thing like that stop him.

"Listen, Mom. Can I call you back? This isn't a good time."

"Why? What's wrong now?"

"Nothing's wrong." Hunter's hands were already on her. On her breasts. He was panting, and she was beginning to.

"Hannah, I don't like this...you up there all alone with a man who is uncivilized...I'm coming up."

The drive would take one hour. Hunter would take longer.

"No...Mother...don't."

"It could be dangerous."

Her mother didn't know the half of it. He was bending her over and she was talking with her head upside down. She hoped her voice didn't sound funny.

"Everything's all right. Really."

"It doesn't sound that way to me. You sound funny."

"I'm...getting a cold. I got a...chill last night."

And more. Ever so much more.

Her knees were already on the floor. Any minute now he would be inside her.

"I have to go now, Mom. Call you later."

The thrust drove her across the rug. Had she got the phone hung up in time?

The first convulsions of pleasure overtook her, and that was her last coherent thought for a long, long time.

"I was beginning to get worried about you, Hannah."

It was three o'clock, she was sitting on her bed with the telephone and Hunter was in the den watching TV.

"I meant to call you back sooner, Mom, but so much has happened today, this is the first chance I've had."

"Good stuff or bad stuff?"

"Good." *Wonderful. Phenomenal. Unbelievable.* And that wasn't just the sex.

"Tell me about it."

"First, how's Dad?"

"I think he's getting better. I really do."

Her heart broke a little. How like Anne to translate her own hopes into an optimistic attitude. If Hannah wanted to look beyond the rosy picture her mother painted, she'd have to visit the nursing home and see for herself.

"I wish I could come for a visit, but right now that's impossible."

"I know, I know. Tell me...how did it go today?"

"Better than I ever thought possible. I wanted to tell him about his family, so I looked up everything I could find on the Internet. The Wolfe family is very prominent...old money from a steel empire."

"He's *that* Wolfe?"

"One and the same, though his parents had become teachers. There was a media feeding frenzy after the plane crash. I printed it all out and read it to Hunter."

"Do you think he understood any of it?"

"All of it, I believe. According to the records, he was a child prodigy. He has a photographic memory and the IQ of a genius. He's in the den now watching CNN, drinking in every word. I thought it would be a good way to bring him up-to-date."

"Or make him want to head back to the wilderness. They don't ever talk about anything except disaster."

"True, but how else is he going to become oriented?"

"All this must be very hard for him."

"It's impossible to tell. He keeps his emotions under lock and key."

"No wonder. Think of it...twenty years without human contact. Has he said anything yet?"

"Not a word."

"Not even a sound?"

Hannah felt her face getting hot. The sounds Hunter made wouldn't do to tell her mother.

Instead of telling an outright lie she said, "I'm hoping that will come with time. I just wish I had some training in this area. I don't know if I can do it."

"You can do anything you set your mind to. You always have, you always will."

"Thanks, Mom. I love you."

"I love you, too, Hannah. Take care, darling. I just wish I could be there to help you."

"You're where you need to be. Give Dad a kiss for me."

"You know I will."

Hannah looked up to see Hunter standing in the doorway. She hadn't heard him. How long had he been there?

"Hi." She smiled at him. "I guess you're getting hungry. How about a late lunch?"

In the time it took her to speak of food, he'd crossed the room, stripped aside her silk wrap and positioned her on the braided rug beside the bed.

"But then I suppose a man who ate as much breakfast as you did won't be hungry again for quite a long time."

Which was fine with her. Very, very fine.

By ten o'clock that night Hannah was exhausted. Combine marathon sex with the stress of trying to cram twenty years of lost family history into one day, and she was more than ready for bed. She was desperate.

She stood in the doorway for a while watching Hunter. He was glued to the TV, gloriously oblivious to how he looked. Better than any movie star she'd ever seen. More like a god. A wild, primitive god.

He wasn't wearing a stitch. In fact, he hadn't all day.

Neither had she, except for occasionally donning her purple silk robe. Why bother? Clothes would have been nothing but a hindrance anyhow.

"Hunter."

He turned at the sound of his name. That was a good sign, wasn't it?

"I'm going to bed now. I have to have some sleep. Okay?"

He didn't say anything, but he didn't turn back to the TV, either.

"Please don't try to run away or anything. You won't, will you?"

Still no response. She sighed.

"Stay in the house tonight. Whether you sleep in your bed is up to you. Just stay here. Okay?"

He was watching her intently. She saw his body language change, saw the fire leap into his eyes. Unconsciously Hannah tightened the belt on her robe.

"I'm too tired to go traipsing through the woods looking for you tonight." She gave a rueful chuckle. "I'm an older woman, you know."

Four years if the newspaper accounts were right. Which meant that when she was sixty he would be only fifty-six, a very young and virile fifty-six, capable of attracting forty-year-olds.

What was the matter with her? By then he would be long gone from Mississippi, and there was no telling where she would be. Nor who she would be with.

She had lots of wild oats left to sow.

She gave a rueful smile. At the rate she was going, she was probably going to run out of oats in the next few days.

"I'm going to bed now. Good night. I'll see you in the morning. Right here." She pointed to the floor for emphasis, and Hunter laughed.

Good God. How absolutely *male* of him.

She wheeled away and marched to her bedroom. She even thought about slamming the door, then decided that would make her look even more foolish.

If there was anything Hannah despised it was looking foolish.

She ripped off her robe and flounced into bed buck naked. She'd thought she would fall asleep the minute her head hit the pillow, but darned if she didn't lie there missing him.

Missing him, for God's sake. Like any ordinary female. Like her sister.

She even found herself dreaming with her eyes wide open, remembering how wonderful it had felt to be held in his arms last night and thinking how great it would be if he were in the bed with her now, holding her, simply holding her.

She heard the plaintive call of an owl from deep in the woods. The moon shone through her window, still impossibly bright and big as a galleon. She could even see Mars. It looked like a red-gold Christmas ornament hanging in the treetops.

Why hadn't she ever noticed all those things before? Well, actually, she had, but they had never looked like this. They had never had such immediacy. They had never felt so *personal.*

She tossed from side to side, sat up and punched her pillow a couple of times, then tried to sleep flat on her back which caused her to snore. Sometimes. When she was extremely tired.

From the den came the faint sounds of the TV. Which didn't mean a thing. For all she knew he could be swimming downriver by now. Or up. North toward Alaska.

She kicked back her covers and tiptoed to the den. There he sat in the dim glow of the television screen. Looking no less gorgeous than when she'd left him.

Hannah tiptoed back down the hall, and climbed back into bed. It was going to be a very long night. She could tell.

Chapter Seventeen

November 7, 2001

I am fixing to get drunk. Skunk-drunk.

I can't take it anymore, that's all there is to it. First, there was all that business with Hannah up there in the woods with a man who has lived with wolves and might do no telling what all to her, then Emily called and said, "I can't get Hannah to answer her phone...Jake and I are thinking of driving down to see her...he's never seen her place," and I made a total fool of myself.

"Wait. You can't do that," I shouted, and when she asked, Why? I said, "Just because."

Like a child. What was worse, I couldn't think of anything else to say. As if I'm the one in the coma.

I never could think of any adequate excuse to give her. I just kept saying, "Hannah's too busy right now, is all," and when Emily hung up she was miffed at me.

Which turned out to be the least of my worries, because when I got to the nursing home I discovered a bunch of complete strangers in Michael's room singing "In the Garden"...if you can call what they were doing singing.

It was dreadful the way they were carrying on. Mournful. Dirge-like. Exactly as if they were conducting a funeral.

"What's going on here?" I asked. "What are you doing in my husband's room?"

I guess I was shouting, and I must have scared them all to death because they stopped their caterwauling. Thank God. Michael hated that song, anyhow.

Hates. Hates. I must think of him in the present.

Well, a wormy-looking little man separated himself from the group and said, "Hi, I'm Ron, and we're from Mt. Pisgah Baptist Church."

He looked so earnest and apologetic I felt like patting him on the arm and saying, "There, there, it's all right."

I didn't, though, because just when I was getting my manners back a large woman in tight yellow bell-bottoms that cupped under said, "I know this is hard for you, Mrs. Westland, but he's going to a better place."

I wanted to slap her. My upbringing was all that saved her.

"My husband's not going anywhere, but you are. Get out of this room. All of you."

I know, I know. That was rude. But I didn't care, not even when two nurses poked their heads in to see what was all the commotion.

Larry Baird himself came down to smooth things over. When he asked me what was wrong I said, "They didn't even get my name right," then I started bawling.

I could tell I was headed for a real crying jag because I could feel my nose getting hot and swelling. It always does when I cry really hard.

"These groups do come here from time to time. Most of our patients and their families enjoy them."

That dried up my waterworks fast, I can tell you.

"Well, I don't, and neither does Michael. He likes Blues. Keep them out of this room."

He lobbied so hard for them I asked, "Are you their agent?" It just flew out of my mouth, and I guess I'll have to think of some nice way to take it back because I certainly don't want Michael to suffer the consequences.

Maybe Clarice can come up with something clever. She's good at that.

Anyhow, when I got home I got in the shower and scrubbed myself hard in case any unctuous residue was still on my skin from that time I'd let Larry Baird hug me.

What in the world ever made me think he was sexy?

Oh, I'm going to make it up to Michael, I can tell you.

But not tonight. I'm afraid to see him, afraid I'll start crying all over again and not be able to stop.

They say don't drink alone, especially when you're in this kind of mood, but I don't know. Clarice would come over if I called. Or Jane. Still, I feel the need to be alone with this misery. I need to look at it from all angles, to figure things out.

Maybe to learn.

I know what Michael would say to me. "Precious, you have to have tears in your eyes in order to have rainbows in your soul."

When I was cleaning out his office I saw a book in his

shelves with a title something like that. A book of Native American wisdom. Michael loved that kind of thing.

He loved books of all kinds—poetry, history, science....

Loves. He loves them....

Oh, God....

Chapter Eighteen

Anne...where are you? A while ago I caught a glimpse of the light. I reached up and tried to hold on, but I couldn't. I couldn't find anything to hold onto, and I kept slipping back.

It's comfortable down here in the dark. Too comfortable. I have to fight to keep myself from settling in. I have to struggle to keep from saying, "Okay, this is fine, this is all I want."

It's not all I want. I want you. I want to come home, but I can't seem to find the way.

Chapter Nineteen

Hannah was dreaming. She was dreaming that Hunter was in the bed with her kissing her. *Kissing* her. And oh, it felt so good, so wonderful....

But wait...his leg was heavy on hers and the mattress sagged under his weight.

This was no dream. He was actually lying beside her with his arms around her and his lips on hers. How could that be?

Where had he learned that? Where? Was kissing natural? *Not in the animal kingdom. Wolves don't kiss.*

But Hunter was no wolf: he was man, all man. Hannah's questions evaporated under the delicious onslaught of his lips...his hands.

My God, what he was doing with his hands ought to be declared illegal.

She was already over the top, and that was before he turned his attention to her breasts. She made whimpering, wanting sounds as he pulled her nipples deep into his mouth. Tangling her hands in his hair, she pulled him closer while explosion after explosion rocked her.

Need was fire in her blood and she became a wild thing, a she-wolf whose only thought was to be filled with him. "Please," she whispered, "please...."

She tried to struggle onto all fours, but Hunter pressed her back to the bed. When he lifted himself on his elbows to smile down at her, she cried out like a petulant child, "No, please...I want...I need...."

Incoherent with passion, she cupped her breasts and offered them to him once more. His tongue was hot, so hot, and she groaned as he stroked and suckled her.

"Yes. Yes...I'm dying...I'm dying...." She arched like a fish under the convulsions that shook her. "Hunter... please...please...now!"

He lifted her hips and entered her. No, not entered. Impaled. That was Hunter's way. No half measures.

Pressed flat against the mattress she could see his face. It was absolutely miraculous, this view she had as he reveled in his latest discovery. Pale light came through the window and fell across his cheekbones, his nose, his mouth. He had beautifully sculpted features. She reached up and traced them with her fingertips, marveling.

"How did you get to be this wonderful?" she whispered, and his mouth curved upward in a smile.

Did he know? Did he understand?

Then all questions left her mind as he carried her over the moon and they crash-landed on her tumbled bed.

"Hmmm, marvelous." She stretched and curled into him, languorous and satisfied, expecting a repeat of their lovely interlude in the woods, bodies pressed close, hearts keeping time, breaths mingled on the chill night air.

Instead he licked the tips of her breasts until she was tingling all over.

"Hunter?" He answered her soft query by sliding under the covers, and when his mouth closed over her, desire swept her once more like fire in a wheatfield.

"There," she said, a woman gone wild. "Oh yes, there...." Then she caught his hair and held him in that good place where nothing mattered except the curve of his mouth, the talent of his tongue and paradise.

A paradise without end, she was thinking sometime later as he stretched flat on his back and lifted her hips over his. And then thought was impossible for she was in flames and he kept pouring on the gasoline...in inventive ways that mystified and astonished her.

She screamed her pleasure to the moon...and then to the sun as it laid pale-pink fingers across the windowsill. Sometime after dawn she fell into a hard sleep, and when she jerked awake a short time later Hunter was gone.

Hannah snatched her robe from the bedpost, and as she streaked past the den the television screen caught her eye.

She stood in the doorway mesmerized. This was not CNN she was watching, but a channel with movies that made her blush.

Then they made her laugh. "And all this time I thought he was watching the news," she said as she flipped off the TV and went in search of Hunter.

Hunter smiled when he heard her coming. She was making as much noise as a freight train. *Funny* how the words were coming back, the phrases. They bombarded him every waking moment, except those times when he could lose himself in her sweet hot body.

"Hunter?" she called. "Where are you?"

He didn't dare call out, not yet. Words still felt clumsy

on his tongue. Early this morning when he'd slipped from her bed he'd gone into the woods where everything felt familiar, and there he'd practiced saying what he'd heard, what he remembered.

He listened to her footsteps on the kitchen tile. "Are you in the house? Oh, please, please be in the house."

She was worried about him. He didn't want her to worry.

He stepped into the hallway just as she came through the kitchen door. She stopped suddenly with her hand over her heart.

"You scared me." Something in his face must have given him away. "No, I mean you *startled* me." She came close and put her hand on his arm. "Please, please don't think you ever scare me, Hunter. You don't. You never have."

That had been obvious from the first moment he'd watched her beside the campfire. He wished he could tell her so. The only way he knew to reassure her was with a smile.

She touched his face. "I think you understand everything I'm saying. Do you?"

How much should he reveal to her? He didn't want anything to change her. She was bold and honest, the way wolves are. Nothing held back. Every feeling expressed. Every thought revealed.

Still, he didn't want her to give up on him. He didn't want her to think that teaching him was impossible. And so he nodded.

Yes. I understand.

"I knew it." Hannah laughed, then cupped his face. "I could tell by looking into your eyes that you understood."

She stepped back from him, suddenly self-conscious, and he was almost sorry he'd revealed the truth.

"What I said in the woods…about *teaching* you…." She

lifted her long hair off her flushed face. "I mean...after last night...."

He stopped her flow of words with his mouth. A kiss. Lovely word. Lovely practice.

Hunter took a long time easing her embarrassment. With his mouth covering hers, his sap rose quickly. The wonder of it all was more than he could bear to think about, and so he didn't think: he acted.

He lifted her off her feet and she wrapped her legs around him; then braced against the wall he entered her. She was instantly hot and ready, which seemed only natural to him.

The wolf always chose his mate wisely, and Hunter had learned from the wolves...and the television.

Chapter Twenty

"I would ask if you're hungry, but I saw that whole pack of honey buns you devoured this morning."

Hannah was leaning against the wall outside her office door, too satisfied to move and barely able to think. One thing was certain: she had to get her mind off her libido and onto the business at hand or she'd never get Hunter ready to reclaim his birthright.

She had her story to write, too, otherwise Jack would be calling to see why she hadn't met her deadline. Thank God she'd lost only one roll of film in the ravine.

"Hunter, what were you doing here when I found you?"

He led the way into the office, went straight to her bookshelves and selected Steinbeck's *Grapes of Wrath*. Several novels already lay open on her desk...works by James Joyce and William Faulkner and Eudora Welty. She'd thought, of course, that reading to him would be a good way to reacquaint him with language, but she'd had something simpler in mind, something that a nine-year-old might have read twenty years ago.

He handed the book to her then put his finger on her mouth.

"You want me to read this to you?"

He nodded, and of course that made perfect sense now that Hannah thought about it. He'd been a child prodigy. He'd probably been reading at high-school level before his parents' plane went down. Possibly even college. *My Friend Flicka* was not for him.

"I think this is a very good idea, but first you have to put some clothes on. You're quite a distraction, you know."

She was looking directly at his most impressive body part, and he laughed. Well, let him. She didn't care as long as he kept doing what he was doing. And if last night and this morning were any indication, there didn't seem to be any danger that he would stop.

Still....

"Here's what I suggest. Let's take a bath, then *get dressed.* You understand what I'm saying, don't you?" Why didn't he wipe that grin off his face? "Well, of course, you do. And I'm not talking about those smelly old bearskins, either. Today you will wear proper clothes."

His grin got bigger, darn his hide. Of course, she could see both the humor and the irony of what she was saying. She started grinning, herself.

"Let me amend that. You'll wear clothes as long as I can keep my hands off you. I'm afraid you've unleashed something wild in me."

He scooped her off her feet and headed toward the bathroom.

"I was talking about separate baths, you know." He bent

down and took her nipple deep into his mouth. "Then again...maybe not."

She wondered what the endurance record was for twenty-nine-year-old males?

Somewhere in the middle of their "bath," Hannah's thinking shifted a hundred and eighty degrees. What had once been unfettered sex and uncomplicated need became an unexpected matter of the heart. Wrapped tightly against Hunter with water sloshing over the side of the tub she understood how Pygmalion must have felt when the ivory statue he'd created changed from an object of beauty to an object of love.

But this was no Greek legend. Hannah didn't have a goddess Aphrodite to magically transform her creation. She only had her own limited resources.

If she succeeded in her mission, then what? What would a man who had spent twenty years in the wilderness do in a society that thought writing a letter was primitive? Her head hurt just thinking about it...and her heart.

What had she done?

Hunter cupped her chin and studied her face, then lifted her out of the tub, wrapped her in a towel and carried her to the bedroom.

"I don't think I'm up to this," she said.

He laughed, then gently placed her on the bed, left the room and shut the door. She was asleep before her head hit the pillow.

Hunter dressed while Hannah slept. The clothes constricted him, but he was determined to wear them for Hannah's sake. And for his own.

He stared at his own image in the mirror, amazed that such a simple act as wearing jeans and a T-shirt had the power to transform him. He felt almost human again.

Some part of him had known that all along, but over the course of years his identity had merged with that of his wolf brothers. They were his protectors, his teachers, his friends. They were a loyal, fearless, loving family—and they were all he had, all he knew, all he'd had any hope of knowing until Hannah came along.

He'd thought of himself as one of them for so long that he experienced a shock every time he caught a glimpse of himself in Hannah's mirror. But it wasn't merely his outside appearance that had changed. He was becoming someone else on the inside, someone with disturbing questions.

Once he'd pondered where he would find his next meal, and now he wondered whether he would ever completely find his way back to civilization. Or whether he even wanted to. If what he'd seen and heard on CNN was true, then he wasn't certain he would ever fit in.

The code of the wolf was simple—loyalty, obedience and fidelity. Those were the rules. Those were the keys to survival.

Wolves never fought over territory; a leader and his mate merely moved on until they found their own. And contrary to the legends Hannah had told him, wolves never killed for the thrill.

How could a society that called itself civilized know less than their brothers in the wild about civilized behavior? In Hannah's world civil disobedience seemed to be the norm.

Hunter went into her office and picked up the photographs she'd taken in Denali—Whitey's son Snow who had become the leader after Whitey's death and Rain, his mate, one of the kindest females Hunter had ever known. Loss and uncertainty almost brought him to his knees.

He'd been one of the most skilled animals in the wilderness, but here he felt as helpless as a newborn. Would his comprehension of the written language return as quickly as his understanding of the spoken language?

He bent over the photographs and traced the dear familiar faces with his fingertips.

"You dressed."

He whirled at the sound of Hannah's voice. She stood in the doorway dressed in jeans and a simple white shirt, her hair long and loose, her cheeks still flushed from sleep. His loins stirred powerfully. He wanted to take her again.

He took a step toward her, and a familiar light leaped into her eyes. She was receptive. The urge to take her on the floor in his customary way almost overpowered him.

Forgetfulness would come so quickly, but confusion merely waited in the background. The minute he left the wilderness he'd set out on a path that he knew would be dangerous.

In the wilderness only the fit survived. In some ways it was the same in civilized society. The only difference was in the training required for survival.

He reached for the book and thrust it into her hand.

"You want me to read?" she asked, and he nodded. "This is a very good idea."

He led her to the sofa and she settled down beside him then opened the book.

"Eudora Welty's short stories…this is great Southern literature. Did you have any idea what you were choosing?"

He shook his head. *No.* And yet, hadn't some sixth sense whispered her name?

"I'm going to start with 'Why I Live at the PO.' It's hilarious, and one of my favorites."

He leaned over her shoulder as she started to read, but he could discover no connection between what she was saying and the words that marched across the page. He put two fingers over her lips.

''What's wrong?'' She smiled when he scooped her up. ''What about our lesson?''

Considering that the mere sight of her aroused him, having her shapely bottom perched so conveniently in his lap caused an immediate response. Her eyes widened and her face softened in a way that was becoming increasingly familiar and dear to him.

How easy it would be to forget about training. How easy it would be pretend there was no world outside the confines of Hannah's cottage.

But another challenge stirred his blood. Years ago, he'd stopped dreaming of the future, yet now it stretched before him, attainable at last…if he could prove himself worthy.

Hunter opened the book then placed her right hand on the page and touched her lips.

''You want me to point out the words as I read?'' He nodded *yes*. ''That's a good idea, a *very* good idea.''

With Hunter leaning over her shoulder, Hannah read until her voice was hoarse. She'd been reading hours, and yet he never lost concentration, never displayed signs of unrest.

''I have to stop awhile.''

He closed the book and stared at her with those molten silver eyes. Suddenly Hannah was all too aware of the heat of his body, of the way it warmed her skin and stirred her blood. Lord, she was beginning to have a one-track mind.

It wasn't merely sex she had on her mind, but the delicious blending of spirits she felt with him…and the more dangerous merging of hearts. She had to stop this before it was too late. Or was it already?

What had happened to that sensible woman who was going to simply enjoy the moment until it came time for

Hunter to leave? What had happened to simplicity and purpose? What had happened to sanity?

He lifted a strand of her hair and let it sift through his fingers. The gesture was natural and so absolutely normal and civilized that for a moment Hannah forgot this wonderfully virile, complex, intelligent man was only one step away from the primitive bearskin-clad wolfman she'd found in the wilderness.

She cupped his face and looked deeply into his eyes. "I want you to know something Hunter Wolfe, I'm terribly proud of you. You've exceeded all my expectations...." A flush crept into her cheeks, and she amended her earlier statement.

"I'm not going to be coy and pretend you don't exceed my expectations with sex...mating, as you knew it with the wolves. Certainly, you do. I never dreamed such pleasure was possible."

He smiled, presenting the perfect picture of a self-satisfied male with a huge ego. Was she creating that bane of women worldwide, a player? Lord, imagine turning him loose on the unsuspecting female population.

A surge of jealousy took her by surprise. She had to get control of herself.

"I'm going into the kitchen and make something for us to eat. Why don't you come and watch? It will be good for your education."

She sounded like a schoolmarm, and he didn't miss a single nuance. His grin proved that.

Hannah jumped off his lap and took a fighting stance, hands on hips, chin outthrust.

"Go ahead and laugh. That's just like a man."

His laughter goaded her, and as she stomped off to the kitchen she realized she was madder at herself than she was at him. She marched to the cabinets and began to slam doors. After all, she had to take her anger out on something, and it most certainly wouldn't be the hunk of primitive pulchritude lurking in her living room.

What was he doing in there, anyway?

She marched to the refrigerator and jerked open the door. It looked like a slaughterhouse. A ton of fish, half a cow and a whole hog stared back at her.

She'd destroyed the entire animal kingdom in order to provide fuel for Hunter Wolfe's delicious body. Hannah was in no mood for meat. She needed ice cream and strawberries topped with a mountain of whipped cream. She needed the kind of food that would put pounds on her hips while she ate. She needed the kind that would make her feel guilty for days after she indulged. At least it would take her mind off the *real* reason she was feeling guilty, the *many* reasons she felt guilty.

She started assembling the world's biggest ice cream sundae, then her skin prickled and her heart beat faster. She didn't even have to look up to know that Hunter was standing in the doorway, tall, bronzed and mouthwatering.

"You probably haven't had ice cream in years." She didn't dare look at him. Looking was too dangerous. "It's rich and fattening. It probably clogs the arteries and does no telling what all to the rest of the body."

Oh, lord. His body....

Her hands trembled, and that made her even angrier. She squirted so much whipped cream that it slid off her ice-cream confection and across the table, then slithered to the floor. It plopped on her bare foot and spattered her ankles.

Why didn't he do something? Why wasn't he laughing?

Hannah risked a peek. The heat of his gaze incinerated her, and she could do nothing but hold the can in mid-air, staring.

He stalked her with the slow, lazy grace of a wild animal certain of his prowess.

"Don't you take a step closer." He didn't smile, didn't blink, didn't even pause. "If you come any closer you'll be sorry."

Why wouldn't he? All he had to do was look at her with those burning silver eyes and she surrendered. He must think she'd gone crazy. As a matter of fact, she was beginning to wonder.

"Hunter...I'm warning you...."

He wasn't the kind of man who heeded warnings. Ever.

Hannah aimed and fired. Whipped cream splatted his face and dribbled onto his shirt. Eyes gleaming, he reached for her. With barely time for one last blast, she aimed for his groin.

His lips slammed down on hers and the can clattered to the floor. Hannah didn't stand a chance. He vanquished her anger in two seconds flat. It took three to conquer her heart and by the count of four he'd captured her entire citadel.

His hands ripped at buttons and hers fumbled with zippers.

"Let me," she whispered, and then they were writhing on the floor and she was licking whipped cream off his eyebrows, his cheeks, his mouth. His delicious mouth.

It roamed her body like a heat-seeking missile. They bumped the table leg and ice cream and strawberries cascaded over them. The combination of cold and heat drove her wild. Inspiration seized her, and she grabbed a handful of berries and scattered them across her chest and downward.

"How about a little dessert before the main course?"

He savored her breasts, then followed the trail of berries to their secret hiding place.

"You certainly are a fast learner," she murmured, and that was the last thing she said for a long, long time.

Chapter Twenty-One

November 15, 2001

It has been five months now since Michael went into a coma, and I want to shout the house down. I want to scream until my throat is raw. Actually, I did. Yesterday I got in the car and drove down the river road until I came to a deserted place, then I climbed on a bluff overlooking the Mississippi and just stood there with my mouth wide open, screaming.

When I told Clarice about it and asked, "Am I losing my marbles?" she said, "No. It's called the primal scream.

Wise people use it. It's like letting steam out of a pressure cooker so it won't blow up."

Clarice knows a little something about everything.

Except coma. Nobody knows much about coma. Nobody can answer my questions.

"When will Michael wake up?" That's what I asked his doctor, and he said, "I wish I could tell you, Anne."

Then I said, "Is he ever going to wake up?" Do you know what he did? He gave me this sad-eyed look, then patted my hand and walked away.

I know I told Michael I would never lose hope. Not ever.

But I lied. I'm losing hope. Here it is nearly Thanksgiving, and I'm facing the prospect of another lonely holiday.

Oh, I know, I know. I'll have my children, but that's not the same as having Michael. In fact, being surrounded by married children and seeing all that bliss makes me even lonelier.

Hannah won't be in Atlanta, of course. Not with that wolfman in her house. Every time I call him that, she reminds me to call him by name, and none too gently, either. She has always been bossy and opinionated, but lately she's been sharp and edgy as well. I don't know what's come over her.

Well, yes, I do. She finally bit off more than she can chew. Though she tells me her pupil is making great strides, he's still not talking.

"At least he's wearing clothes now," she said when I called last night. "He's eating with a fork, too."

I thought I detected just a hint of territorial pride in her voice, the kind you get when you've staked your claim and are feeling frisky and sexy and just plain wonderful....

I had to stop writing and cry because I'm wondering if I'll ever feel that way again. I'm wondering if I'll ever get Michael back.

Naturally, I jumped to conclusions where Hannah's

concerned. She's far too sensible to lose her head over this wilderness man.

And yet, it would take a man just that extraordinary to capture her attention.

I wish I could drive up there and see for myself. I wish Hannah would let me tell Daniel. He has such a level head. I would feel better if he could come over here and assess this situation. Hannah nearly bit my head off when I suggested it.

"Don't you dare tell Daniel."

"Why not? He'd certainly never tell."

"For one thing, I don't know how Hunter would react."

"What else?"

"What do you mean, what else?"

"You said, for one thing. What's the other reason you don't want Daniel to visit?"

"Because...this is something I have to do myself. I got Hunter into this, and I'm going to get him out."

"How do you propose to do that?"

"When he's ready, I'm going to let him make his debut into polite society."

"Just how polite?"

"I'll start small...with a family gathering."

"You said he wouldn't be ready for Thanksgiving. I think Christmas would be a little overwhelming."

Thinking of family occasions reminded me that Michael and I have an anniversary coming up on December 10, and right out of the blue I started to cry. On the telephone. Of all the embarrassing things.

Hannah thought it was her fault.

"I'm sorry, Mom," she said. "I didn't mean to upset you. I wasn't thinking. I'll take Hunter somewhere else for his first outing...."

"It's not that," I said, and when I mentioned our anniversary she said, "Maybe Dad will be back by then. Maybe that's just the incentive he needs to come back."

"Do you really think so?"

She must have heard the doubt in my voice, for she said, "Mom, we can't lose hope. We can't ever lose hope."

She's right.

I'm going to carry my blue gown to the nursing home, the one Michael loves, and I'm going to sleep with him tonight. I'm going to wrap my arms around him and say, "Darling, do you remember our wedding night? Do you remember what you told me? Anne, you said, all our nights together will be just this wonderful...for the rest of our lives."

Michael always loved a challenge. I'm going to remind him of that promise and dare him to keep it.

Chapter Twenty-Two

Hannah drifted through her days, isolated by necessity and cocooned by love. There, she'd admitted it. She loved Hunter Wolfe. She loved every aspect of him...the primitive wolfman, the eager student, the insatiable lover, the laughing companion, the mysterious man hidden inside a deep and abiding silence.

And that made her work with him even harder. Now instead of knowing that she acted solely on what was best for Hunter, she had to wonder if every decision she made was based on her own selfish interests.

She would ask Hunter, but he couldn't speak. Or wouldn't.

And Lord only knew where he slept.

Not in her bed, though he came there every night. And as soon as she began to drift off, he eased out the door. She'd stopped following him weeks ago.

For reasons known only to him, Hunter was going nowhere.

Did he stay because of her? She didn't dare ask herself that question. And she certainly couldn't ask him.

Disgusted with herself, Hannah flung back the covers then shivered when she put her bare feet on the floor. She raced to the bathroom and was just reaching for her robe when the phone rang.

"Happy Thanksgiving, Sis."

Was it Thanksgiving already? She'd forgotten.

"Good morning, Daniel."

"Morning? It's two in the afternoon."

"Oh."

"Hannah, are you sick? Mom's worried about you."

"I'm fine, Daniel. I just overslept, that's all."

Her robe slid from her shoulder and bared a breast still rosy from Hunter's tender attentions. Hannah sank onto her bed and lay back against the pillows, still dreamy from the wee-hours marathon that had lasted until dawn.

"That's not like you."

"I've been working hard."

Daniel snorted. "You can do the work of three people with one hand tied behind your back. Something else is wrong. I can sense it."

She'd have to be careful. She and her brother were so close that he could almost read her mind.

"What has Mom been telling you?"

"Nothing. She said you couldn't come to Atlanta because you were involved in research and couldn't get away, but I'm not buying it."

"It's the truth." *Mostly.* She hated lying to her brother. What if she told him?

Then he'd tell Skylar, and some nosy reporter snooping around to catch the sexy singer in candid shots with her preacher husband might overhear. It would be all over the paper and the whole world would descend on them.

Hannah didn't dare risk the truth. "How's Skylar?"

"Are you changing the subject?"

"Yes."

Thankfully, Daniel was always eager to talk about his beautiful, talented wife, and so Hannah got off the hook.

"She's got everybody in the parish eating out of her hand."

"I knew she would. They just needed a little time to get used to the idea of change, that's all."

"Change?" Daniel laughed. "Skylar is not *change*. She's a firestorm."

His happiness overflowed, and suddenly Hannah's heart hurt. Could she be jealous? Not that she wanted the same things he did...three children and a mortgage. Still, there was something to be said for knowing that when you wake up in the morning the person you love will be right there at your side. There was something to be said for knowing that any time the thoughts that breed in darkness scare you, you can reach out and anchor yourself to a dear, familiar body.

"Are you sure you're all right, Hannah?"

"I'm great."

"All right, then. You know you can call me if you need me."

She was going to be crying any minute now. That would really send up flares.

"I've been taking care of myself for years. I could whip ten of you, Daniel."

"All right. That's more like it...here's Sky. She wants to talk."

"Hannah!" Skylar's voice washed over her like music. "We missed you today."

"I missed you, too. Sorry I couldn't join you."

"I was thinking about Christmas...."

Hunter appeared in the doorway without his beard, and Hannah dropped the phone. Never taking her eyes off him, she picked it up.

"Sorry. The phone slipped out of my hand. What were you saying?"

Flame leaped into Hunter's eyes as he strode to the bed. Without preamble he dropped to his knees, pushed aside her robe and buried his face in the place she most wanted him to be.

"I was saying that I'm going to be doing a Christmas concert tour, and Daniel's going with me. Is it all right with you if we move the family celebration up a couple of weeks?"

"Yes...oh, yesss."

Hunter plied his talented tongue, and Hannah grabbed a handful of sheet and stuffed it in her mouth to muffle her moans.

"Great. Emily wants to have it at her house, but I thought we might plan it at Belle Rose so Anne won't feel so displaced."

Hunter stood up and shucked his shirt and jeans. As he came back toward her, Hannah caught her breath.

"Sky, can I call you back later about this? Something has come up."

Something magnificent. She caught his hips, then closed her mouth around him.

Christmas was a long way off, but this...*this* was so immediate, so splendid.

He pushed her back against the pillows, and she wrapped her legs around him.

"I'd like to keep you like this forever," she whispered.

Then a hurricane swept over her, and she laced her arms around him and hung on.

Hunter welcomed the sweet hot storm that enveloped him. As always, forgetfulness came quickly. He lost himself in her. The daily plague of questions ceased and his inner turmoil quieted.

Here in her bed. Here in her body.

Gauging her readiness, he plunged deep, and she rewarded him by arching like a speared fish and screaming her pleasure. He never tired of being with her, watching her, listening to her.

I'd like to keep you like this forever, she'd said, but he knew it was an impossible dream. Somewhere outside this small house in the woods by the river, the truth waited. The real world was out there. *Her* world. And it wouldn't be as gentle as she. It wouldn't treat him as kindly.

Twenty years ago he'd been cast into the society of wolves. If CNN painted a true picture he was going to be cast into another one, only this time the wolves wore three-piece suits and silk ties.

His brains and his courage had rescued him the first time, but it was his ability to adapt that saved him. Could he do it again?

And did he want to?

Here…now…buried deep in Hannah's hot flesh while she moved beneath him like a river, he wanted to shout, *Yes!* But what of tomorrow?

It was time. Time to find out. Time to reveal himself.

Passion built in him until he couldn't contain it. With a cry he remembered from long days and lonely nights in the wilderness, he spilled his seed. Then he rolled to his side with Hannah caught close against him.

Hunter buried his face in her fragrant hair and whispered her name.

She jerked back and stared at him. "What did you say?"

"I spoke your name. Hannah."

"I can't believe it…I can't believe it…." She traced his lips with her fingertips. "That was perfect, wonderful." Tears filled her eyes and spilled down her cheeks. "All this time…you could talk."

"No, not at first. You wouldn't have called my early attempts speech."

"You practiced?"

"Yes."

"But I never even heard you."

"I didn't want you to hear me. I practiced in the woods."

"So that's where you've been going every night?"

"Yes."

She sat up and propped against the headboard. He loved that she didn't pull the sheet up to cover herself.

"How did it happen? When?"

"Some of the words began to make sense to me when we were still in Denali. Once we arrived here and you bombarded me with language, it all came back very quickly. Vocabulary. Grammar. Syntax."

He cupped her face. "You're a magnificent teacher, Hannah."

The lovely color that flooded her cheeks fascinated him. So did the sudden tightening of her nipples. Unable to resist, he raised himself on his elbows and lavished his attention on them.

"In many skills," he added, and she tangled her hands in his hair and held him close.

He felt his hold on reality slipping away. He was losing himself once more, drowning in Hannah.

"There's so much I want to ask you," she murmured.

"Later." He rolled her over, and she anchored herself to the bedpost as he drove home. "Much, much later," he said, then a riptide washed him away.

Chapter Twenty-Three

Afternoon sun poured through the bank of west-facing windows in the kitchen. Hannah and Hunter sat at the table surrounded by remnants of a Bohemian feast—broccoli, cauliflower and carrots along with every kind of fruit in the refrigerator served with mounds of whipped cream. Though she'd grown up celebrating a traditional Thanksgiving in the bosom of her large and loving family, she counted this the best Thanksgiving she'd ever had.

And all because of Hunter Wolfe. He had the kind of face that should be sculpted in marble and displayed as a national treasure. With his beard gone, she saw the high cheekbones, the aristocratic nose, the strong, square jaw.

"I can't stop looking." She reached out and traced his cheekbones. "Nor touching."

"I enjoy it. But I guess that's obvious."

"Yes." She dipped a strawberry in the cream to cover her discomfiture. Now that he could talk she felt slightly off-balance and a bit embarrassed. Thinking back over their sexual exploits of the past few weeks she decided she was the one who needed civilizing.

She was miffed at herself. She'd always been in control. *Always.*

"Hannah, look at me." He cupped her face. "Don't let my ability to speak change you."

"I never believed that anything or anyone had the power."

Something flickered in the depths of his quicksilver eyes. Confusion, probably. If she weren't careful she was going to ruin weeks of work. And all for nothing.

What good would it do to bare her soul? What good would it do to tell a man who knew nothing of romance that she finally understood what her mother had been talking about all these years. You don't find true love, it finds you.

Confessions would distance him and possibly drive him away completely. Lack of transportation and destination wouldn't stop him. A man who had survived twenty years in a wilderness would find a way.

"Can you talk about what happened in Alaska, Hunter? Do you remember?"

"Yes, I remember...all of it." A shadow crossed his face.

"I'm sorry. If this is too painful, you don't have to talk about it."

"I'll have to eventually. From what I've seen on TV, the press won't be as easy as you are."

"True. Once this story hits, you'll be bombarded with questions."

"If I stay."

Hunter dropped the bomb and it lay between them, ticking. The truth was out and there was no way to take it back. Now everything she said, everything she did would be tempered by the knowledge that she could light the fuse and blast the ground from beneath her feet.

He scooted his chair back, and she saw it as a symbolic gesture. He was already pulling away from her. Soon the student wouldn't need the teacher. Soon he'd be on his own.

"When the plane went down I remember thinking, we're all going to die."

He began telling his story quietly, and she leaned forward in order to hear. She wanted to reach out and touch him, to hold his hand or grip his arm, anything to anchor herself, anything to anchor him.

"I don't know what happened after that," he continued. "I don't know how they died. All I know is that when I regained consciousness I was in a cave surrounded by wolves...and I knew my parents were dead."

"How frightening that must have been for you."

"Yes. I was afraid. But I was also hurt and weak from lack of food and water."

"How far were you from the plane?"

"I don't know. Years later when I went back, I tried to calculate. I think the wolves dragged me about three miles."

"Amazing."

"Not when you consider that it was late winter and huskies, which are most like their wolf brothers, can pull enormous loads over snow. A nine-year-old boy would have been a cinch for six wolves."

"I didn't know anything about wolves or wolf behavior," he continued. "I figured they had eaten my parents and were getting ready to eat me."

"I highly recommend it," she said.

The minute the sassy retort was out of her mouth she

wished she could take it back. But there it was, as bold as his conversational bomb.

His smile was lazy and knowing. "We can arrange that."

"Then I'd miss the story."

"The story can wait."

She didn't protest when he ripped off his pants, nor when he reached for hers. She offered no resistance when he positioned her on the floor and drove into her. Hannah anchored herself to the leg of the table and shouted her pleasure to the waning sun. And her relief.

She was selfish to the core, taking what she needed without regard to Hunter. As he pounded into her she kept telling herself that he was receiving as much pleasure as she, but a small insistent whisper kept saying, *You're the one who needs this, Hannah. You're the one who needs to hold on.*

What was she going to do when it was time for him to go? How would she survive after she sent him off to reclaim his rightful place in society? How could she breathe without Hunter?

Her fear made her greedy, insatiable. Or was it merely the man?

As if he'd read her mind Hunter scooped her up and spread her on the table among the broccoli and the strawberries. Fruit and vegetables flew in every direction as he ravished her, starting with her breasts.

Every inch of her skin was sensitized. Every bone in her body ached for him. He teased her diamond-hard nipples with teeth and tongue, and when she caught his hair and strained closer, he pulled them deep into his mouth and suckled.

She was going to stay on that table forever. She was going to close her eyes and pretend twenty years in the wilderness had never happened. She was going to immerse herself in ecstasy and never resurface.

"Yes, yes, yesss," she murmured, and then when he left her breasts, she moaned, "Nooo."

He smiled at her. "I'm not finished with you yet."

"Goody."

His chuckle was deep and sexy, his tongue hot and hard as it left a burning trail down her body. She wrapped her legs around his neck, and when the spasms overtook her, she reached for support and landed her hand in the whipped cream, going soggy and warm.

Hunter reached for the bowl, smeared cream on her breasts, then started all over again.

"I wouldn't have survived that first winter if it hadn't been for the wolves."

Hannah kissed his hand and cuddled it to her cheek.

They were sitting on the sofa in front of a fire he'd built. Sometimes he thought he could never get enough of the toasty warmth, and other times he felt as if he might suffocate. This was a night for warmth.

Hannah lay against his chest with her legs stretched along the length of the sofa. Her silky robe was loosely belted and fell open so that he could see the play of firelight against her skin.

He couldn't get his fill of looking.

"This reminds me of that night in Denali," he said. "The time I saw you beside the campfire."

She tried to twist around to face him, but he held her tight. "Don't move. I like you like this." He chuckled. "I liked you that night, too."

"I don't know what came over me."

"Don't you?" He slid his hands under her robe and ran his fingertips across the soft mounds of her breasts.

"Of course, I do. I was just being coy."

"You're bold, Hannah. Always be bold with me."

When she didn't reply he resumed his story. "I didn't see the wolf pups at first. The mother brought them to me one by one then lay down beside me while they fed. Every now and then she would nudge my face with her nose."

Memories swamped him, and he had to stop talking.

"She fed you?"

"Yes. I was injured and too weak to leave the cave. It wouldn't have done me any good anyhow…a nine-year-old boy without adequate clothing nor a single weapon trying to find food in three-foot-deep snow."

"It took enormous courage to do what you did, Hunter. And a powerful will to survive."

He tightened his hold and kissed the top of her head.

"I regained strength quickly, then the alpha male started bringing me meat. I threw up the first time I ate raw elk."

"But not the second?"

"No. I had no weapons and no skills to survive the wilderness in winter. I learned to eat like a wolf, to live like a wolf and to think like a wolf."

"All that time the search party was looking for you not three miles away. Did you think you would be rescued?"

"Yes. At first. Especially after the snows melted. I learned a lot that first summer. I applied what I'd learned in Scouting plus what I was learning from the wolves… how to stalk small game, how to sense danger, how to travel downwind from the enemy and how to camouflage my own scent so it wouldn't betray me."

"They stayed with you, then?"

"I went with them," he laughed, remembering. "They insisted."

"How does a wolf insist?"

"When the pack got ready to move, Whitey would catch

my hand in his mouth and tug. He was the alpha male, the pack's leader. I had names for all of them by summer.''

''With his stamp of approval, the rest of the pack had to accept you.''

His admiration for her went up another notch.

''You're right...you did your research before you went to Denali.''

On the long flight home, she'd told him about her assignment there, never knowing that he understood. And he'd witnessed at close range the passion she brought to her work, the passion she brought to everything she did.

''I do thorough research before I undertake a new assignment.'' She caressed his thigh. ''Usually.''

''I'm glad you made an exception with me.''

This time when she swiveled to look at him, he didn't protest. She gazed deeply into his eyes...and beyond. Her gaze penetrated his heart, his soul.

''What made you stay so long?''

He'd wondered when she would ask the question...and how he would answer.

''Hunter,'' she traced his face. ''You don't have to answer if you don't want to. It's none of my business. Really.''

That's when he knew he would tell her the truth, or as much of it as he could. He wasn't sure he even knew the whole truth. What man is ever certain of his motives?

''You know I could have found my way out?''

''That's obvious. Any man who could survive the wilderness for twenty years without benefit of any modern convenience or commercial trapping, let alone modern medicine, is bound to have figured a way out. Especially a man with the IQ of a genius.''

''That first year I kept thinking I would be found. The

next I was too busy figuring ways to survive to invest any time and effort in finding a way out.''

"And after that?"

"For the next few years I tried to walk out...as soon as the snow melted. I was young and scared...I always turned back."

"You were in one of the most remote sections of Denali," she said. "Nobody went there much until about three years ago."

"I was fifteen before I saw another human being. I wouldn't have survived those six years without the wolves. They were more than my protectors. They were my teachers, my friends, my family. By the time the trapper invaded our territory, I had become a wolf."

"When I first saw you in the moonlight, I thought you were a wolf."

"I had taken on their posture and their habits. Though I could never learn to speak their language, I did learn to communicate with them."

"How?"

"I used gestures, but mostly our communication was telepathic."

He didn't elaborate. That part of his life was still too private, too personal.

He remembered the year he'd turned fourteen how Whitey had seemed to understand his longing for a companion of his own. He was coming of age, his sap was rising, and he had nowhere to turn.

Whitey had encouraged a liaison with one of the young females in the pack. Hunter had politely declined, but that year he realized he would soon have to leave the pack and make his own way.

Fortunately for Whitey, he didn't leave that year....

"The year the trapper came everything changed," he told Hannah.

"I never knew his name. I didn't know about his steel traps until one of the young females in the pack got caught. She'd lagged behind the others in a hunting party. We were too busy with the young moose we'd brought down to miss her. Finally Whitey missed her and we backtracked, but we were too late. By the time we got there, the trapper had already taken her."

"How horrible for you."

"More horrible for Whitey. He got caught in one of the traps. I was able to free him, but that day I came to view man as my enemy."

"I understand," she said, though nothing in her experience had prepared her for dealing with a man who had stayed so long with the wolves that his identity was linked to theirs.

Would the bond ever be broken? Would Hunter ever truly embrace her world?

"I didn't try to leave anymore after Whitey got caught. The wolves needed me, and finally I'd found a way to repay them."

He didn't speak for a long time. Instead he buried his hands in her hair then let it sift through his fingers.

What was he thinking? What secrets was he keeping?

Hannah didn't dare ask. She had to let him tell his story in her own way.

She'd heard of kidnap victims identifying so strongly with their kidnappers that they would do things they would never otherwise have done. Become criminals, even.

How much more strongly Hunter would have identified with the animals who had saved him, succored him and loved him.

Then there was the element of fear. Even people in safe

environments sometimes feared change. For Hunter, leaving Denali was not merely change, but a complete metamorphosis.

"Over the years I saw only two more men, both trappers. If I had revealed myself, they might have led me out. Or they might have killed me."

There was another long silence. The fire burned low; the logs crackled and split.

"I discovered I didn't want to be found. I didn't want to leave…until you came."

He turned her onto his lap, and as he bent toward her Hannah wrapped her arms around him and held on, held on tight.

Chapter Twenty-Four

December 1, 2001

I'm marking the days on my calendar until our anniversary. I don't know why. Michael has not shown the least bit of progress, not the tiniest sign that he's getting ready to come out of his coma.

"Anne, it has been six months," Clarice told me on the phone this morning. "If you keep going to the nursing home day and night, you're going to end up in the hospital."

"Which hospital?"

"Whitfield."

The state hospital for the insane.

Sometimes I feel as if I'm already there...watching old movies with a comatose man, flirting with him, cajoling him, sleeping with him. Trying to seduce him, for heaven's sake.

I'll do anything to get him back. *Anything!*

"I can't stop," I told Clarice, and she said, "I know. I just worry, that's all."

And then because she's such a good friend who always tries to encourage me, she said, "Medical science is coming up with new cures every day."

"I don't think coma is something you cure."

"You know what I mean."

Of course I did. I was just being ornery, is all. If Michael stays in his coma I'm going to need an attitude adjustment or nobody will be able to stand me.

"I have two tickets to the theater tonight," Clarice told me. "I'll pick you up at seven-thirty and I don't want to hear any argument."

Michael used to love the theater. We had season tickets to the community theater, and every time we traveled to Boston or New York we would always try to see a few plays.

I think the renewal notice for this year's season tickets came last month. I tossed it in the garbage can.

What does that say about my state of mind? If I'm not careful I'm going to become a dried-up, thin-lipped pessimist. I don't even want to think about it.

"What's playing?" I asked Clarice.

Cat on a Hot Tin Roof.

That certainly describes me to a T, but I didn't say that to Clarice. She must be so tired of me dwelling on my own troubles all the time. My children, too. I'm even tired of myself. I've become a boring woman, somebody with a one-track mind.

"Okay, but I have to go by and see Michael."

"Before or after?"

"After, I think."

That way I can stay, but I didn't tell Clarice. She

would try to talk me out of it. She thinks I'm not getting enough rest.

But I can't bear to make a brief visit, as if Michael is nothing more to me than a distant relative...or even a stranger, the kind of poor forgotten soul good church-going people visit out of compassion. Or pity.

Michael hates pity. That's one thing I won't do. I will never pity him. No matter what. No matter if he stays....

Oh, I won't even think about that possibility. I need to focus on bringing him home.

There must be something I haven't tried, something that will blast him out of the safe cocoon of deep sleep and make him want to come back to me. Make him *come back to me*.

I glance at the calendar. Nine more days till our anniversary. I remember the one we spent in San Francisco three years ago. Michael had to go for a conference of high-altitude filmmakers, and I went along because I love being with him. Anytime, anywhere, but especially in that romantic city on the west coast.

The day of our anniversary he slipped out of his meeting early. We drove along the coast and stopped at beaches along the way to admire the view, but mostly to hug and kiss and admire each other. Oh, we were so in love.

Are. We *are* in love.

We stopped to watch the sunset and although it was December and the water was cold, we pulled off our shoes, rolled up the legs of our jeans and cavorted in the waves.

Our feet got so cold we buried them in the sand, then wrapped my red cape around us and watched the most beautiful sunset I've ever seen.

Or perhaps it wasn't. Maybe it was beautiful simply because Michael was there, holding me close.

Afterward we had dinner at our favorite restaurant high in the mountains, cold noses, wet jeans and all. When we got back to our room Michael put on our favorite blues CD and we danced to our song. "Wonderful Tonight." The song that perfectly describes how it is with us...always wonderful.

We made love all night. I'm not exaggerating.

We are still insatiable. Even at our age.

Oh, I can't possibly let him go. I can't possibly let Michael remain lost from me.

Tonight I'm going to take the music box, the one we found in San Francisco two days after our anniversary, the one that plays "Wonderful Tonight."

If Michael doesn't respond to that, I don't know what will bring him home. I just don't know.

December 2, 2001

I'm so exhausted I can barely sit up...and so excited I can hardly hold my pen.

Last night when Clarice and I went to the nursing home after the play, I said, "Michael, darling, I've brought something for you to hear."

I wound up the music box and set it on his pillow, then stood beside his bed holding his hand. I would have stretched out beside him if Clarice hadn't been there.

But I'm glad I didn't. I might have missed what happened next.

I was standing there holding onto him while Eric Clapton sang our song, and all of a sudden Michael's eyelids began to quiver.

"Clarice! Do you see that?"

She hurried over, but by that time Michael had already stopped. I thought I was going to have a heart attack. I couldn't be imagining things. Not again.

"Michael, can you hear me?" I squeezed his hand. "Blink, darling. Blink if you can hear me."

I held my breath while we both watched. At first there was nothing. I simply couldn't take another disappointment. Any minute I was going to burst into tears.

I leaned down and kissed his lips. "Michael, darling," I whispered. "Please come back to me. *Please.*"

His eyelids quivered again. Clarice and I both burst into tears, and she said, "I'm going to get the doctor."

"It's late. I don't think he'll come."

"He'll come if I have to drag him here by the hair of the head."

I don't know what she said, but within thirty minutes the doctor was there.

"It's a very good sign," he said after I told him what had happened.

He stayed an hour, waiting for Michael to blink again, but there was nothing. (Lord, if I could afford it I'd send him a brand new Mercedes. That's how grateful I am.)

"Movement of the eyelids is usually one of the first signs that a patient is coming out of coma. Sometimes they come out quickly, and sometimes they take days."

"But he is coming out, isn't he?"

He put his hand on my shoulder and squeezed. "Anne, I wish I could say that for sure, but I can't. Every case is different."

Clarice wanted to stay, but I told her, "I want to be with Michael alone."

"You call me if he wakes up. I don't care what time of night it is."

He didn't, though. I sat by his bed all night watching. Just in case.

He didn't blink all night. Not unless I dozed and missed it. And I don't think I did.

How can I sleep when my beloved is trying to return to me?

Chapter Twenty-Five

Anne, are you still there? You must be. I smell the fragrance of your perfume. Jungle gardenia. God, how I love it.

Reach for my hand, my precious. Hold onto me. Don't let go.

I'm trying to come home.

Chapter Twenty-Six

The phone brought Hannah out of a deep sleep. The first thing she noticed was that Hunter was not there.

The second thing she noticed was that the clock said five.

She picked up the receiver, and, before she could even say hello, her mother said, "Hannah, he moved his eyelids."

"Dad?"

"Yes! Last night. Right after 'Cat on a Hot Tin Roof.' It was very late or I would have called you, but this morning I said to myself, This is the kind of news that can't wait."

"Mom, slow down. Take a deep breath…now, tell me everything from the beginning."

Her mother told her about putting the music box on his pillow and sitting up all night in case Michael woke up.

"What does the doctor say?"

"He's cautiously optimistic."

"I'll drive down this afternoon."

"What about Hunter?"

"I have good news, too. He's talking."

"In complete sentences?"

Hannah laughed. "I don't see what's so funny about that."

"Sorry, Mom, I'm not laughing at you. I'm just happy, that's all. He's very articulate. Remember, he has a brain that would be the envy of Einstein."

"I'm happy for you, darling, but I don't want you to come."

"Why not? Hunter will be fine here alone for a few hours. I have to start doing it sometime, and it might as well be now."

"I know this is going to sound selfish, but I don't want any of my children here."

"If you're trying to protect us because you think it might be a false alarm, forget it, Mom."

"I told Daniel not to come, too. And I'm going to tell Emily the same thing…Hannah, I want to be alone with him when he wakes up."

A few weeks ago Hannah would have argued, but that was before she'd met Hunter. Now she understood her mother's reasoning. A heart-connection such as her parents' was a beautiful, private thing, almost sacred. Their reunion should not be shared.

"I understand, Mom. Call me the minute Dad wakes up, no matter what time it is."

As soon as Hannah hung up, she grabbed her robe and went in search of Hunter. He was on the front porch curled in a wool blanket asleep on the floor.

She started tiptoeing across the porch, but the minute her foot hit the planks his eyes flew open.

"I didn't mean to wake you up." She knelt beside him, and he pulled her into the cocoon of blanket.

"Did you really think you could sneak up on me?"

She laughed. "Silly, wasn't it?"

"You're never silly, Hannah."

"Hunter...you miss Denali, don't you?"

"Sometimes."

"Is that why you're sleeping out here?"

"Sometimes I feel trapped inside. Besides, luxury is making me soft."

"Not that I've noticed."

Laughing, he slid his hands under her robe and traced a line of fire down her inner thighs. Heat licked along her skin and she melted. It amazed her that one touch from him could do that.

There were plans to make, things to say. She couldn't keep getting sidetracked.

"We have to talk," she said.

"We will." He shifted, then caught her taut nipple between his teeth and began a gentle tugging.

"We really have to talk."

"Go ahead, I'm listening."

His tongue flicked in hot little circles, and even as she said, "I mean it," she wove her fingers through his hair and pulled him closer.

"I'm so easy," she murmured.

"I'm so glad."

He lifted the blanket over them, and they didn't come out for a long, long time.

They were in the kitchen finishing breakfast. Hunter chuckled when she gave him a soft dreamy look over the rim of her coffee cup.

"What's so funny?"

"You're easy to read."

"I like to think of myself as inscrutable."

"You're not. You never have been. I could read you the first time I ever saw you."

Hannah was not the blushing kind, and it always surprised and delighted him when she did.

"Anyone could have read me. What I was thinking was perfectly obvious."

He remembered the firelight on her skin, the crisp cold air and the pull of the moon. He remembered the quickening of his pulse, the rush of passion and the howl that rose in his throat.

Instinctively he'd suppressed it. Instinctively he'd known...what? That she would change his life forever? That life as he knew it would cease?

The prospect both excited and terrified him. He must not let his terror show. The wolves had taught him that. If he could keep the lessons of the wild, he would be all right. He would survive.

But was it enough for him merely to survive? Once he would have said *yes.* Now he had no answers. Only questions.

"Let's talk outside," he said.

She understood that this talk needed to be made in his territory, not hers. She understood that the things they would say would surely end their idyll in the woods and that he needed to be free when he said them and not confined between four walls that sometimes felt like a prison. All these things she knew.

And yet part of her rebelled. Part of her wanted to crawl back under the blanket and lose herself once more in the pleasures of the flesh. The world's greatest panacea.

She wanted to live in her pink cocoon of love and never come out. Instead she said, "All right," then took his hand

and followed him out the door and through the woods. He didn't stop until he came to the bluff overlooking the river.

Even then she couldn't talk about the thing that was on her heart, on her mind. She couldn't bear to say the word, *future*. She had to hold onto the present a little longer.

"I think my dad's waking up."

"That's good news, Hannah. Will you go to see him?"

"Not yet."

"You can go. I won't leave."

"I didn't think you would."

A breeze lifted her hair and whipped underneath her sweater. Hannah wrapped her arms around herself, but it wasn't the wind that made it cold: it was the idea of losing Hunter. It wasn't the simple fact that he no longer held her hand; it was the terrifying realization that she'd almost finished her job and now she had to let him go. She had to give him a chance to claim his birthright and make his own way in the world.

I don't want to.

The truth whispered through her mind. Of course she didn't want to, but unless she set him free the teacher/protector would become the jailer; the safe haven would become a prison.

"I think you are ready to face society," she said.

"I know."

"I don't plan to toss you out and see if you sink or swim. I thought I would introduce you to my family first, do a sort of test run."

"And if I pass the test?"

"For starters I think we should look up the Wolfes and announce that you are alive...before we notify the news media."

"I think that's a sound plan."

"Good."

They both faced the river. Why didn't he look at her? Why didn't he touch her?

"You said *we.* Does that mean you'll be with me when I announce that I didn't die in the plane crash that killed my parents?"

Hannah crammed her hands in her pockets. "I'll be there."

"For how long?"

Finally he turned, and she could no more resist the pull of his gaze than she could resist him.

"For as long a you want me...."

The silence stretched for miles, and then he pulled her into his arms.

"I want you, Hannah."

Chapter Twenty-Seven

December 3, 2001

Everybody has been so good to me—Clarice, Jane, all the staff here at the nursing home. They've all helped me keep a round-the-clock watch on Michael. His eyelids quivered again yesterday for about two minutes as if he's trying really hard to come back to me.

Clarice is the one who set up the watch.

"You can't stay here twenty-four hours a day," she told me yesterday when I refused to leave his side.

"What if he wakes up and nobody is here? What if he decides just to go back to sleep?"

"You can't do it all, Anne."

"Maybe I was wrong not to let the children come."

"There's no sense in all of them driving to Vicksburg when I'm right here with nothing to do. Besides, the more time I spend here, the more I can see Larry Baird."

"The nursing home's director?"

"Don't look so astonished. He thinks I'm sexy."

"How do you know?"

"A woman can tell, that's all."

She's right, but I didn't tell her about my personal experience with him. Not that I think he's sleazy. Now that all that's behind me, and I don't have to worry about going off the deep end with him—or any other man for that matter—I see Larry in a different light.

He is kind of attractive in that off-beat way Clarice likes.

She left about twenty minutes ago, but I notice her car is still in the parking lot. She said something about taking a peek into his office to see if he's still here. Maybe he is. Maybe he invited her to dinner. I hope so.

Clarice is one of the most loving, giving people I know. She deserves somebody to love her right back.

While I was at Belle Rose I changed into a red party dress. For Michael. Because he has always loved this color on me. Because I want his homecoming to be a celebration.

Clarice didn't comment. I knew she would understand.

I'm so tired I can hardly see to write anymore.

I need to rewind the music box. Ever since the first sign that Michael was trying to wake up, I've had "Wonderful Tonight" playing. I want him to have that constant reminder of our remarkable love.

I've talked to him almost non-stop, too. Over and over I say, "Michael, I love you. I love you, darling. Come back to me."

I've talked so much my voice is hoarse, and now I'm talking with my heart.

"Wake up, my darling," I'm saying. "Wake up and come home. I'm waiting...."

Chapter Twenty-Eight

Anne? I hear you, my precious. I feel the weight of your head on my chest. I smell the fragrance of gardenias in your hair.

I want to touch you, but my hands won't move. I can feel them, though. I can feel my whole body. I feel the blood flowing through my veins and hear the sound of my own breathing.

I'm holding onto these new sensations, and I'm holding on tight.

The darkness keeps trying to draw me back. It's a seducer, this deep, dark sleep. It's a curtained room untouched by the mundane and filled with treasure chests that hold the answers to all the great cosmic questions.

Down here I know the secrets of the sea, the truth of the stars and the lessons of a single dewdrop. I converse with kings and Caesars and pharaohs. I am wise beyond Solomon.

I would stay in my safe cocoon except for one thing: you are not here.

I want to see the way you bite your lower lip when you're thinking and the way you toss your hair when you know I'm in the room. I want to watch you knotting a towel around your waist when you emerge from your bath and putting perfume on the pulse spot behind your knees.

I want to come home, Anne.

My eyes are too heavy to open, but I'm trying...I'm trying....

Is it morning, Anne? Is that sunlight I see coming through the window.

I can see!

"Anne?"

I touch your hair, caress your cheek, and I know beyond a shadow of a doubt that the entire universe is contained in your slender body.

You lift your head and look at me. "Michael...oh, God, Michael, you're awake."

We reach for each other, and I can taste your tears. I promise myself I will never make you cry again.

Chapter Twenty-Nine

Hannah was at her computer typing while Hunter bent over a notebook writing his name. How long had it been since he'd held a pen in his hand?

In Denali, he'd used a rock to scratch marks on the cave walls. At first it had been a way of keeping track of the days, then later it had become a method of keeping track of his life. First he'd used words. Then as the sound and the cadences of language faded, he'd turned to pictures.

Now as his mind wandered over the past, he began to doodle, and then to draw. When he'd filled one page he turned to the next.

Hannah looked up at him and smiled. "How is it coming over there?"

"I'm getting the hang of it," he said. "How about you? How are you doing with your story?"

"This piece on the wolves is probably the best thing I've

ever written. It helps to have the source sitting on my sofa."

The way she looked with her head tilted and her hair sliding over one cheek stole Hunter's breath. His pen began to move rapidly over the paper.

"Don't move," he said.

"Why?"

"Just don't move."

Suspicion leaped into her eyes. "Hunter, what are you doing?"

"Just a minute and you can see...don't move."

"Are you drawing?" He was too busy trying to capture her on paper to answer. "Hunter...you're sketching!"

She jumped out of her chair, and when she looked over his shoulder she gasped.

"It's just a doodle," he said.

"It's magnificent."

She reached over and took the notebook from him, then carried it to the window where she would have natural light. As she studied his drawings, Hannah got more excited by the minute.

She hadn't slept well for days. Ever since Hunter had started talking, really. Her thinking had ranged from guilt to absolute terror. Squirrel-like, the thoughts whirled round and round in her mind: I've brought him out of the wilderness and civilized him, and now what will he do?

His education had stopped when he was nine, never mind that he was a genius. His skills were suited to the wilderness (and the bedroom) instead of the boardroom, and he was as unfamiliar with the ways of commerce as he was with the ways of Martians.

Now she saw a faint glimmer of hope.

She sat beside him on the sofa. "How long have you been doing this?"

"Since I was a child."

"Before the plane crash?"

"Yes."

That made sense. To all accounts, his mother had been a gifted musician. He had strong artistic genes.

But these were not childlike drawings, nor the sketches of someone who hadn't drawn since the age of nine. These were powerful and sophisticated in ways that Hannah couldn't explain.

Still, she had to remember that she was dealing with a man with a giant IQ.

"Did you take lessons as a child?"

"No. My mother thought they would stifle my natural style. She believed that artists should be mature and confident in their own talent before they let someone else try to teach them. Musicians are the exception, of course."

"And you haven't sketched since then, since childhood?"

"I didn't say that...I kept it up over the years."

"How?"

"Cave drawings. I used a sharp rock."

"Oh my God...the cave...that day you tried to get me to follow you inside. That's what you wanted to show me."

"That, among other things."

The way he smiled heated her blood and stole her breath.

"If we don't focus on the issue at hand, we'll never come to any decision about your future."

His smile ratcheted up her libido several notches. And when he leaned over and whispered in her ear, the notebook slid to the floor.

"Yes," she whispered, and he picked her up and carried her into the bedroom...by way of the kitchen. They left a trail of clothes from the door to the bed.

He slithered an ice cube over her breast, then took the

chilled nipple deep in his mouth. Speared by pleasure, she arched upward murmuring, ''Please, please, please.''

''Not yet, Hannah...hold on...hold on.''

She cupped her breasts, offering them up to him with soft whimpers, and he suckled so deeply the earth stopped spinning on its axis. The entire universe held its breath.

''Don't stop,'' she whispered. ''Don't ever stop doing that.''

''What about this?''

He slid the ice down her belly then warmed the cold flesh with his tongue. And when she felt the sensations of cold followed by heat inside her, she shattered into a million pieces.

''Now, Hunter....''

''Yes...now.''

He lifted her hips with both hands. Impaled, she hung over the edge of the universe, screaming her pleasure to the stars.

It was a long, long while before they came back down to earth. Curved against him, warm and sated, Hannah twisted his long hair around her fingers.

''I was thinking about your sketches. You have a remarkable talent.''

''Thank you.''

''Your work would sell.''

''I've been gone too long to know.''

''It's something you could do, something that wouldn't require schooling or computer skills or any of those things you've missed over the years.''

He rubbed his knuckles against her cheek and she wondered how much of what she was saying had to do with considerations of his future and how much had to with her own selfish motives.

She wanted to keep him. Oh, she wanted to keep her wonderful wolfman.

"We can get you some art supplies," she added. "I have a friend who owns a gallery in New York. I could send some photographs of your work up to her."

When he didn't say anything, she sighed. "I know, I'm moving far too fast. You haven't even ventured out in public yet. Then there's the matter of notifying your relatives and the press conference and...."

A loud ringing interrupted her flow of words. Hannah picked up the receiver and said, "Hello."

"Hannah...." Her mother started to cry.

Hannah sat up, pulling the sheet over her breasts as if she'd been caught red-handed.

"Mom? What's wrong?" More sobbing. "Mom?"

Hunter sat up beside her and rubbed her shoulders. "What has happened?" he asked.

"I don't know...Mom...."

She heard muffled sounds, and then another voice. "Hannah...."

"Oh my God...Daddy? Is that really you?"

"I can't get your mom to stop crying."

"Well, just hold onto her. She has lots of tears saved up...." Hannah wiped at her own wet cheeks. "What happened? When did you wake up?"

"This morning. We wanted to call all of you sooner, but a team of doctors rushed in and put me through a battery of tests."

"And?"

"I came through all of them with flying colors. It's Anne I'm worried about."

"Just let her cry it out, Dad. She'll be all right when you get her back to Belle Rose...I can't wait to see you."

"Give us a few days alone first, okay?"

Envy pricked her. Hannah had to readjust her image of herself to include selfishness and jealousy. How could her parents love such a daughter?

"Sweetheart, I have to let you go. The physical therapist will be here soon and we want to call Emily and Daniel to let them know we'll be home in a few days...God, that sounds so good."

"'Bye, Daddy. I love you."

"I love you, too, sweetheart."

"See you soon."

As soon as she hung up the phone she collapsed against Hunter, and he enfolded her. It felt so good to have someone to hold on to. It felt so good not to *have* to be strong.

Chapter Thirty

December 7, 2001

How can a heart hold this much happiness? Michael's back and I want to shout it to the moon. I want to run through the streets naked and yell at the top of my voice, "My beloved has returned. My husband has come home again."

And he is home again. All the way.

I've heard of people who woke up out of comas disoriented. Some of them even with bits and pieces of memory missing. With whole sections of their past wiped out. With family members turned to complete strangers by their long journey into darkness.

But not Michael. He came back all the way. He came back like the cavalry with the flag flying. At full mast.

Oh, thank God, thank God.

When we got back to Belle Rose we locked the doors and took the phone off the hook.

"I'm glad you wore that party dress, Anne," he said, and I told him, "I wore it just for you. To celebrate."

"Let's celebrate," he said.

I told him, "I don't want to wear you out."

"I've been resting up for this. Wear me out, Annie."

We spent our passion quickly, then lay in bed till dark holding each other.

Lord, I can't stop touching him. I can't stop looking at him.

Actually, I'm afraid to stop. I'm afraid he'll slip back into a coma if I don't keep watch.

That first night when he woke up and caught me staring, he didn't say a word, just took me in his arms and held on. I was so relieved to discover that he'd actually been in a normal sleep instead of a coma that I started crying all over again.

"I'm sorry," I whispered, and my wonderful, intuitive Michael said, "That's all right, darling. You've been strong long enough. It's safe to cry now."

I finally cried myself out, but I still haven't been able to sleep. I still worry that Michael will fall back into that dark and scary sleep that held him captive for six months.

Six months can be an eternity. I suppose there are people who emerge from tragedy stronger and wiser. I don't know if I'm one of those people. Maybe it's too soon to tell.

I do know that I have a heightened awareness of each moment. Sometimes I think we become onlookers of our own lives. We are not truly present except in those times we consider special.

Now I see the webbed feet of ducks and the magic wings of bumblebees. I can tell the call of the cardinal from the song of a lark. I know the earth is made of the dust of fallen stars, and a single rose can hold truth in a fragrant cup.

It's nearly midnight now, and I can't make myself sleep. Except in the daytime when Michael's awake and holding me in his arms.

From my window I can see Saturn and Jupiter vying for brilliance with a full moon. Michael woke up a little while ago and saw me sitting here.

"Anne?"

"Don't get up, darling. I'm okay. I just want to record every precious moment since you woke up."

He got up anyway, this wonderful, magnificent husband of mine. He held me for a while and kissed me, and then he went downstairs to make us some hot chocolate.

But before he left he said, "I'm not going anywhere, my precious."

He's as patient as a saint with me. Sometimes I wish he'd get mad. I wish he'd say, "You look like a sleepwalker. You're going to ruin your health if you keep carrying on this way."

That's what Clarice said yesterday when she called and I told her what had been going on here.

It's so normal, this quick sharp truth that pricks the skin without damaging the heart. I want to have that again with Michael. I want to wake up and be grouchy without worrying that he will be sorry he ever came out of the coma.

I want to grab a handful of my hair that went gray almost overnight and say, "This is all your fault."

I want to shout at him, "You didn't have to go to that mountain. You stole six months from me, from us."

There, it's out in the open. I've finally admitted that a part of me blames Michael for what happened. I can't tell him that. I can't blurt out to the man I love more than life itself, "I'm furious because you left."

Maybe someday I can find a way to tell him, a gentle, loving way that won't assign blame, a soft way that will allow me to empty the hurt so that I can truly heal.

Chapter Thirty-One

Michael was standing on the front steps of Belle Rose watching for Hannah's car to come up the long, winding driveway. When she first spotted him, she cried.

She wiped the tears away with her left hand, and then started waving. He bounded down the steps and scooped her into a bear hug as soon as she opened the car door.

"Daddy, I can't believe you're finally home."

"I can't either. Let me look at you."

He felt thinner, and he wore a nursing-home pallor, but his smile was still the same. His whole face lit up, making his eyes look as if they were dancing.

Hannah studied him for signs that part of her father might be missing. Maybe there was something he hadn't wanted to tell her on the phone in front of her mother.

"Are you sure you're all right, Daddy?"

"The doctors said yes, and I passed Anne's tests with

flying colors.'' He chuckled. "You're tougher than they are, though. I might not fare so well under your scrutiny.''

"Who was the first man to climb Mt. Everest? George Mallory or Sir Edmund Hillary?''

"Who?'' he asked, and she might have panicked if she hadn't seen his eyes twinkling. "You know what I always say, 'It's not who got there first, but who came back.'''

"I'm so thrilled you're back.''

She hugged her father again and hung on. Anne came to the front door, and the minute Michael saw her, he bounded up the steps and wrapped his arm around her waist. She leaned into him and rubbed her cheek against his, and Hannah started to cry all over again.

"I didn't mean to do that,'' she said.

"It's all right. Your mother cried for three days.''

"Two and a half. I'll have you know my children now look upon me as a Rock of Gibraltar, Michael Westmoreland. I won't have you ruining my reputation.''

"That's not the way I plan to ruin your reputation, Mrs. Westmoreland.''

He bent down to kiss her, and Hannah slipped discreetly away. They were still kissing when she got inside the house. With their eyes glowing and their faces turned up to each other, they looked so young that Hannah's heart ached.

She was seeing love at its finest. She was seeing two people who had loved each other from the moment they'd met, soul mates who had spent a lifetime living for and loving each other.

She thought of Hunter and the way he'd made love to her before she left…on the riverbank early this morning, the two of them wrapped together while the sunrise painted their skins pink and gold. Afterward, they'd raced through the woods and climbed into a hot tub in order to warm up.

She loved him. She'd known that for a long time. But would he ever love her? Would he ever feel as if his soul and hers had been created at exactly the same moment, and that the stars had decreed they should be one? Would she ever hear him say I love you?

"Hannah?" Her mother was standing in the doorway, alone. "I didn't mean to startle you."

"That's all right. Where's Dad?"

"He's gone around back to fire up the grill. I told him we'd fetch the steaks from the kitchen."

"Steak? I didn't expect such a feast."

"Daniel and Skylar are coming."

"So, the steak is for Daniel?"

Her mother did a double take until she saw Hannah struggling to control her laughter. Anne swatted her with the dishtowel.

"Make yourself useful. Start counting out the silver...for five."

"What about Jake and Emily?

"They won't be here until tomorrow."

"I'm sorry I'll miss them."

"You're staying only today, then?"

"Yes."

"Is it because of Hunter?"

Hannah felt the heat creep into her face, and Anne didn't miss a thing. The steak pan clattered onto the table as she sank into a chair.

"Oh my Lord," she said. "You're in love with him."

"How did you know?"

"It shows all over you...I should have guessed...all those times when I called and you sounded so...flushed."

"Do you think Dad will notice anything? I don't want to worry him with this."

Anne pursed her lips, then set about rearranging the steak that had scattered across the pan.

"I won't have you acting as if Michael is some kind of invalid. Do you hear me, Hannah?"

"It's not that, Mom, it's just…I don't know."

"I do. Just because your father has lost his tan and is not yet in shape to climb a mountain, you see him as diminished in other ways."

Anne plopped the last steak into place and whirled toward Hannah with her hands on her hips. "Well, I'm here to tell you he's not. He's better than ever." Now her own face got hot. "He's still head of this household, and there will be no secrets."

Relief flooded Hannah. "He's really all right, isn't he, Mom?"

"Yes." Anne's smile made her look like a thirty-year-old. "He's better than all right. He's magnificent…and he's home." Anne fanned her face with her right hand. "Oh Lord, look at me…getting ready to cry again. Michael's going to get disgusted and wish he'd never come back."

"Not a chance, Mom. If Hunter looked at me the way Dad looks at you, I'd own the world."

"Doesn't he love you, Hannah?"

Hannah remembered their leave-taking. *I don't want to leave you here alone,* she'd told him, and he'd said, *I won't leave you.*

Did that mean while she was in Belle Rose? Or forever?

"I don't know," she told her mother. "I don't know if I ever will."

"Give him some time, Hannah." Anne handed her the pan of steaks. "Why don't you carry these out to Michael?"

"I thought you were going, too."

"I want to make the salads…by myself."

Her mother was giving her an opportunity to talk to her dad alone. She leaned over and kissed Anne's cheek. "Thanks, Mom."

"Don't hold anything back from him," Anne called after her.

Outside Hannah paused for a moment to watch her father at the grill. It was such an ordinary sight, one she'd seen hundreds of times growing up, and it reassured her in ways that all her mother's words could not.

He turned at the sound of her footsteps on the flagstone patio.

"There you are." His smile faded as he looked beyond her. "Where's Anne?"

"In the kitchen. She wanted to give us a chance to talk."

"Shoot." He tossed the steaks on the grill then turned to her. "I'm listening."

And he was. From the moment Hannah told him about discovering a wolfman in the wilds of Alaska, she had Michael's complete attention. More than that, she had the benefit of his wisdom and a blessed affirmation.

"You did the right thing, Hannah. To let him be captured like an animal would have been cruel. He would have fought, and possibly died."

"I never thought of that...you're right, Dad. He certainly would have fought. He's fiercely proud and independent."

"He sounds extraordinary. I'll do everything I can to help him, Hannah."

"Are you and Mom having an anniversary celebration?"

"Yes. Clarice wants to give a huge party, but Anne and I have decided we'll keep it small this year. Only family."

He smiled at her. "And Hunter, if you think he's ready."

"I think so. Dad, I don't want the others to know. It won't be a true test if they make allowances for him."

"I agree." Michael turned the steaks, then took a big

swig of iced tea. "Once, when Anne brought steak to my room, I actually thought I was in my own backyard grilling. It was the smell, I think."

The expression on his face told Hannah he was not looking at her but inward to a time and place none of them would ever fully comprehend.

"I'm glad it's not too cold for this," he added, and she said, "So am I."

But she wasn't thinking of backyard picnics; she was thinking of making love on the riverbank.

"I think you're even more beautiful than when I last saw you."

"What?" She gathered her rampaging thoughts. "I'm sorry, Dad. I wasn't paying attention."

He studied her in the intense way that always made Hannah and her siblings believe their father could read minds.

"Is there something else you want to tell me, Hannah?"

She was getting ready to expose her heart, when Daniel and Skylar came onto the patio.

"Dad, I want you to meet my wife. This is Skylar."

As Michael folded his son and the daughter-in-law he'd never seen into a tight embrace, Hannah thought how lucky she was. Both Daniel and Emily had gone through one of the major events of their lives without Michael...their weddings.

Though she had no desire for marriage and all the trappings, Hannah couldn't imagine not being able to share the most incredible discovery of her life with the man she considered a cross between Solomon and Santa Claus.

There would be time for talk later. Anne joined her on the swing glider, and they watched while Daniel and his wife had their joyful reunion with Michael.

"I remember hearing your beautiful voice," he was telling Skylar. "When Daniel told me he was going to marry you, I remember thinking that the woman with the voice of an angel was the perfect match for my son.''

''You were right, Dad. She is.''

Michael studied them both, then said, ''I can see that.''

''Daniel and I were thinking that since you missed our first ceremony, we'd have another just for you.''

''What a wonderful idea.'' Anne left the glider and slid her arm around Michael. ''Don't you think so, darling?''

''This means the world to me,'' he said.

''We're leaving in a couple of weeks for Skylar's holiday concert tour, and you two need some time together. How does next spring sound?''

Michael was so full he could merely nod, and Anne asked, ''Here? In Belle Rose?''

''No,'' Skylar said. ''We want to renew our vows in Atlanta…in Daniel's church. I'm not sure his parishioners have ever forgiven me for marrying their minister in a pagan ceremony on the riverbank.''

''They adore you.'' Daniel kissed his wife. ''Almost as much as I do.''

''Pagan, my foot,'' Anne said. ''It was one of the most spiritual ceremonies I've ever seen. And I'll go tell them so.''

The family roared with laughter, and Daniel said, ''You go get 'em, Mom.''

''She'll box their ears if she has to,'' Hannah told Skylar, and she was only half kidding.

To all appearances her mother was demure, sedate and ladylike. But let one of her own be threatened and she became a tigress. When Emily was eight, Anne had actually told a hulking soccer coach that he wasn't going to have any red left in his hair if he didn't back off and stop bullying her daughter, that if he ever made Emily cry again in PE she was personally going to snatch him bald-headed.

"I thought she might settle down while I was gone," Michael deadpanned, "but I came back to the same hellion."

Anne shot back at him, "You haven't seen anything yet."

They got lost in each other and so were Daniel and Skylar. Hannah was the one who noticed the steak was charring.

Michael rescued it while Anne assured him, "We'll scrape off the burned parts." But Hannah saw the worry that crept into her mother's face.

Late that evening, when she told her parents and Skylar goodbye, she said, "Daniel, walk me to the car."

"Sure thing, Sis."

"Don't call me Sis."

Hannah made the retort more for old time's sake than out of any pique. They left Michael leaning over the piano while Anne played and Skylar belted out, "Blue Skies."

"I'm worried about Mom," she told Daniel as soon as they were out of earshot.

"She looks tired."

"It's more than that. Did you notice how she watches every little move Dad makes? It's as if she's afraid something might be missing and she has to be vigilant to fill the gaps."

"Could be. I think she's just afraid of losing him again. These last six months nearly killed her."

"I know." She squeezed her brother's hand. "I'm glad you and Skylar are staying."

"Sky wants to help Mom put together the anniversary shindig. I wish you could stay, too."

"No can do, big bro."

"What's the hurry?"

She almost told him. She and Daniel had always confided in each other. She was the one he had come to when he'd fallen so inappropriately in love with Skylar. Or so he'd thought, until Hannah had set him straight.

If she could talk to him, maybe Daniel could set her straight. But how? Who would ever understand the absolute foolhardiness of falling in love with the wolfman she was trying to tame?

No one would ever tame Hunter. Of that she was certain.

"I have to finish the story," she told her brother, and it was the truth. But only part of it. The other part was that she couldn't bear to be away from Hunter. And not merely because she worried about what he might decide to do.

She hugged her brother, then drove by the mall on the way home to pick up art supplies. Then she turned her car north toward home. North toward Hunter.

Chapter Thirty-Two

Reclining amid their recently tangled bedcovers with the sheet draped over her hips, Hannah looked over her shoulder at Hunter. He stood barefoot in front of a huge canvas working at a furious pace. Oil paint spattered his chest and the front of his jeans.

"Take your time," she said. "I'm in no hurry."

She enjoyed watching him paint. In fact, it was one of her greatest delights. Hunter brought the same intensity to the canvas that he brought to their lovemaking. She had chosen wisely in buying large canvases. He was a larger-than-life man.

"I want to capture that wanton look on your face while it's still fresh," he said.

"We could do it all over again."

The mere suggestion aroused him. Eyes gleaming, he started toward her.

"I was just kidding," she said.

He propped one knee on the bed and leaned over to brush one nipple with red paint.

''Were you?'' he said, moving the brush to the other nipple.

''Not really,'' she whispered.

The brush clattered to the floor as she pulled him down to her, and it was a very long time before Hunter got back to his painting.

As he posed her once more she looked at the painting he'd already done leaning against the wall—Hannah emerging from her bath.

''If you keep painting me nude, you'll never get all those canvases filled.''

''I had much rather fill you…tilt your chin down a little.''

''Like this?''

''That's good.''

''Hunter, are you nervous about tomorrow?'' They would be driving down to Belle Rose for her parents' anniversary celebration.

''No. I'm looking forward to it. If conversation lags I can always talk about how to steal a grizzly's coat for the winter.''

She loved it that he had a sense of humor. He would do well tomorrow. In addition to his own natural charm and humor, he had aced everything she'd taught him, including the finer points of dining.

Soon he would have no need for her. Not as a teacher and protector. Not as a playmate, either. Certainly not after America's long-stemmed beauties got a gander at him.

''Hannah, what's wrong?''

''Nothing.''

''Is it my hair? You're afraid it will offend your family. I'll cut it.''

"No! Don't you dare. I adore your hair."

"I haven't seen hair like this...except on the covers of those historical romances in your bookshelves." His eyes were twinkling.

"Fabio." She gave an over-the-top sigh. "My secret passion."

"I'll capture him and send him up to live with my wolf brothers for a while."

Though he was still teasing, something inside Hannah clenched as if she were holding on...and holding on tight. The pull of the wild was still strong with him. Someday she would have to give him the choice: do you want to stay or do you want to return?

But not now. Please, God, not now. *Please, please, please....*

She had to have a few more days with Hunter, a few more weeks.

And then she could let him go. Couldn't she?

"Tomorrow when we go down to Belle Rose, I'll start to teach you to drive the car."

"Why?"

"A car will give you the freedom to come and go as you please."

"That's what feet and legs are for."

"I'm afraid you can't run on freeways the way you could race around Denali."

"That's the reason Americans are fat. I'll fly where I'm going and take taxis when I have to."

"I should have known you'd have it all figured out with that big brain of yours." She laughed. "I think I'll limit your TV viewing time. It's giving you some bad impressions."

"All except the X-rated channel."

"You graduated a long time ago."

"Did I?" He put his brush down.

"Hunter, get that look out of your eyes." His bare feet made no sound as he came toward her. "Hunter...." She sighed his name one more time, and that was all.

Before they left for Hannah's home, she said, "You look great. Like a Bohemian artist."

It wasn't his looks that worried Hunter. It was the very real possibility that he would do or say something to cause her distress and make her wish she'd never taken him to meet his family.

He knew pack behavior. He understood that those who broke the codes of conduct were driven out.

"Tell me about your family's rules," he said.

Hannah turned her attention from the road to look at him. "There are no rules."

"Every pack has rules. They are necessary for survival."

She didn't correct him. She didn't point out his lapse into primitive thinking. She merely turned her face back to the road and said, "I see."

He watched the scenery whizzing by. He hated being in the car. For one thing he couldn't make out landmarks. For another he couldn't smell anything. How could he locate the enemy without sight and smell?

He didn't say any of these things to Hannah. Enemies were predators who would pounce when you let your guard down. The only difference between her world and his was that in his world he could smell them coming before they bared their claws.

"Fifteen minutes and we'll be at Belle Rose." She'd told him about the antebellum house with the cannonball still lodged in the wall. He could barely remember his parents' house. All he had was a vague recollection of large spaces and a huge backyard.

She reached across and squeezed his hand. "Just be yourself, that's all. And if you start feeling uncomfortable or…trapped…just let me know and we'll leave."

"Thank you, Hannah, but that won't be necessary." He had no intention of failing the test with her family.

Hannah was the last to arrive. She'd planned it that way. In one sweeping glance she would see the initial reaction of her entire family.

She parked the car beside her brother-in-law's BMW, then turned to Hunter and said, "Showtime." She smiled when he got out of the car and came around to open her door.

"So far, so good."

"If I pass the test, do I get a reward?"

"You get a reward whether you pass or not." She moved into him for a quick, hard kiss, then stepped back and took deep breaths. She was more nervous than he.

"Let's go," she said.

Her family was gathered in the living room, and when they walked in, it was Michael's reaction she watched first.

He sized Hunter up, alpha male of the pack taking the measure of the newcomer to see if he posed a threat to the rest of the members.

Lord, now she was thinking like Hunter. She stifled a nervous giggle.

"Hunter…." Anne came forward and took his hand. "Can I get you something to drink? We're having Pinot Grigio. Or I can get iced tea, a cola or water."

"I'll have wine," Hunter said.

Anne shot a triumphant look toward her daughter, one that said, "You did it!" She hurried off to get the drink, and Hannah watched the rest of the family. Except for Anne and Michael, not one of them knew Hunter's background.

And so far, not one of them appeared suspicious that he was something other than he seemed.

Of course, they'd only got past the introductions. The real test was yet to come.

It was the family's athlete Jake who started the ball rolling. Judging by Hunter's fitness and deeply tanned skin, he correctly sized him up as full of athletic prowess.

"You must be a fellow outdoorsman," he said. Hunter acknowledged this with a smile and a slight nod. "Which sports do you enjoy?"

Hannah held her breath, waiting for his answer. Michael seemed poised to step in if he had to.

"Long-distance running, primarily."

"Ever done any competitions?"

"No. But I've had to run for my life a few times." Hunter's laughter turned a truthful statement into jest, and Jake joined in.

Emily came to stand beside her husband. "So Hunter, where are you from?" she asked.

"I was born in New York, but I've spent most of my life in Alaska."

Hannah began to relax, and then Jake asked, "There are some great ranges in Alaska. Have you ever done any mountain climbing?"

Anne turned white, and Michael hurried to her side. Emily poked her husband in the ribs. "Jake, let's not talk about that."

"I forgot, honey." He hurried over to his mother-in-law. "I'm truly sorry, Anne. I didn't mean to resurrect painful memories."

"That's all right," she murmured, but everybody could tell it wasn't.

Good lord, Hannah thought, did her mother still blame Jake for Michael's coma? After all, he had been the one to ask him to come out of retirement and go back to the mountain. But Michael was a professional high-altitude filmmaker. Or had been. The whole family had lived with the possibility of avalanches and other natural disasters for years.

A deafening silence fell over them. Hannah wished she had never brought Hunter. It was the wrong time, the wrong place. Obviously her family still had wounds to heal.

Why hadn't she taken him to a good restaurant, instead? Why hadn't she done something simple like that?

Wearing the serious look he always got when he was getting ready to deliver a sermon, Daniel moved away from the piano where he'd been standing with Skylar.

"Wait." Michael put a hand on his son's shoulder. "Let me."

When he strode to the center of the room, not a single person watching had any doubt that Michael Westmoreland was back in charge. Not that he had ever been a dictator, but he had been their wise leader and benevolent advisor—the rock that provided shelter for them all.

"In this family we've lived with the capricious nature of mountains all our lives. Especially Everest...the one that nearly killed me."

Anne put her hand over her mouth to stifle a sob. Michael gave her a look of such compassion, such love that she tilted her chin up and returned a brave smile.

"That's my Annie," he said. "That's my girl." He looked around at his family once more. "I know these last few months have been hard for all of you. With the exception of Anne, I think Jake must have suffered the most."

Emily leaned her head against her husband's chest, and he stroked her back.

"I want all of you to know that I went back to Everest because I wanted to. For no other reason." He smiled at his wife. "And Anne, I want you to know that I'm never going again. One climber in this family is enough."

"I have my skillet handy in case you change your mind," she said, and everybody laughed. Anne Beaufort Westmoreland had her spunk back.

"One more thing," Michael added. "No subject in this family has ever been taboo, and we're not going to pussyfoot around the subject of mountains."

"Hear, hear." Daniel lifted his glass. "I propose a toast to Michael and Anne Westmoreland, the world's greatest parents."

Emily chimed in with, "Most of the time," and Hannah added, "When they could catch us."

Then Michael lifted his glass. "To my precious Anne, the love of my life."

She linked arms with him saying, "To my darling Michael, my heart and soul."

The festive mood lasted through dinner, and afterward Emily said, "I don't want to steal Mom and Dad's thunder, but Jake and I have an announcement."

One look at Jake's face told Hannah what her sister's announcement was going to be.

"I'm pregnant," Emily added.

Excitement ran high. Hannah was the only one who didn't join in. All she could see was her once-unconventional sister settling into mundane routine.

"Congratulations," she said, and that was all.

She loved her family and was happy for her sister. She really was. But she was even happier that her sister's news had once again deflected attention from Hunter.

He was doing a superb job of blending in, but when Skylar asked him, "What do you do?" he was stumped for the first time that evening.

"He's an artist," Hannah told her sister-in-law.

And it was true. He had enormous natural talent that she was hoping would translate into a career.

If he decided to stay....

"Hannah?" Her mother lifted one eyebrow.

"Sorry, Mom. What did you say?"

"Skylar's going to sing for Michael and me. Are you and Hunter ready to go back into the den?"

"Certainly."

Hannah squeezed the arm Hunter offered, and he leaned down to whisper, "How am I doing, teacher?"

"Better than I am," she whispered back.

Skylar sang love ballads while Michael and Anne sat on the sofa with their arms around each other. Emily leaned back in Jake's arms and he caressed her still-flat abdomen.

The music made Hannah dream of glorious days and magical nights with Hunter, but she scrupulously avoided looking at him or touching him. She didn't dare. He was so totally uninhibited about sex she couldn't possibly risk arousing him.

And that was all it took—one look, one touch. For both of them.

"My last number is one that is special to both of you for many reasons," Skylar said. "It's 'Wonderful To-night.'"

Michael stood up and pulled Anne into his arms, and they danced while Skylar sang. Afterward Anne suggested a stroll through the rose garden.

"This December has been so mild we still have a few stragglers in bloom," she said.

Everybody declined the walk except Hunter and Hannah.

The veil of evening had fallen over the garden, and when Hunter reached for her hand, she felt electrocuted. Her parents led the way, and under cover of darkness he drew her hand against him.

Sucking in a sharp breath, she looked up at him. His eyes gleamed silver in the moonlight and danced with mischief.

Hannah jumped apart from him when her mother started talking. She and Michael had stopped beside a pink rose that looked white under the stars.

"This old-fashioned floribunda is the only one still blooming," she said. "There's really not much to see in the garden. I just felt the need for air."

"Why don't we leave you two alone out here?" Hannah said. "Anyway Hunter and I need to be going."

"You won't stay the night?" Anne said.

"I think it's best this way, Mom."

Michael shook Hunter's hand. "I'm glad you came with Hannah today. You're an impressive young man."

"Thank you, sir."

Hannah nearly burst with pride. In addition to everything else, Hunter had absorbed her quick lesson in Southern courtesy and manners.

"If Anne and I can help you in any way with your adjustment, all you have to do is call on us."

Hannah hugged both parents an extra long time.

"It was a beautiful evening," she said, "in every way."

As she and Hunter left the garden, Michael and Anne disappeared inside the gazebo.

"I like your family, Hannah."

"They like you, too."

Hannah pulled away from Belle Rose and they didn't talk again until they were on the river road going home.

"Did I pass the test?"

"With flying colors."

He grew quiet for a while, and then he said, "I should have let you teach me to drive."

"Why?"

"Because if I were driving I'd stop the car in that thick grove."

"Why?"

"I want to mate with you."

Without a word Hannah swerved the car onto the dirt lane. Hidden amidst ancient oaks and massive magnolias, Hunter stripped off their clothes and positioned her on the forest floor. As he drove into her, he lifted one single cry to the moon.

Chapter Thirty-Three

December 25, 2001

Christmas in Hawaii! I can hardly believe it.

It's all Michael's doing. A big surprise. When I started trying to plan Christmas around everybody's schedules, he said, "Anne, the children are starting families of their own now. Let's let them create their own Christmas traditions."

"How can we have Christmas without a gathering at Belle Rose?" I said, and he told me, "We won't. We're starting a new tradition."

Then he pulled out two tickets to Hawaii. I whooped and hollered and hula-danced till Michael begged me to stop. He was laughing so hard he swore he was about to split his sides.

This is a dream come true. I've been wanting to come here for years, but Michael was always off on a mountain somewhere or one of the children had a major emergency or Mother was getting married again.

It just never happened, and frankly I didn't know how this trip would work out, being away from home at Christmas and all, but I'm here to tell you that I love it! Every sun-filled, magical moment.

Lord, I feel like a teenager! Michael and I eat coconut straight out of the shell and drink exotic beverages that take the top off my head. Every night we walk hand-in-hand along the beach. Last night we found a deserted spot and wrapped a blanket around ourselves and made love standing up. He mounded sand up for me to stand on so I would be tall, then dug himself into a pit so he would be shorter. It wasn't a very successful way to make love, but the forbidden thrill of it all made us giddy. We laughed all the way back to our cottage.

Oh, the cottage we rented is lovely. It has a thatched roof and coconut trees outside the window. Strange and exotic birds serenade us while we lie under our mosquito netting as naked as the early Polynesian natives.

I'm sleeping like a baby now...and have been ever since our anniversary celebration. I will never forget how magnificent Michael was, standing in the middle of the room taking command. I fell in love with him all over again.

I told him so that night after everybody was in bed, and he said, "Anne, I plan to make you fall in love with me every day for the rest of our lives. And that's a promise."

It's a promise he has kept. Whether he's leaning against the doorjamb playing blues on his harmonica or sitting naked on a towel while we picnic on the floor or leaving a mustache of shaving cream around my mouth from an early-morning kiss, I fall in love with him all over again.

Oh, God, I don't want this to ever end. Even when I'm a hundred I still want to be falling in love with my Michael.

Chapter Thirty-Four

Hannah and Hunter spent Christmas at her cottage in the woods. They saw in the New Year on the bluff overlooking the river, making love under a tent of warm quilts.

A few days later she sent in her story on the wolves of Denali. The remainder of the month passed in a blissful blur. When she wasn't posing for one of his paintings, they were making love.

She knew her fairy-tale existence had to come to an end, but she held on as long as she could. After all, Hunter had to get enough paintings ready for a show, didn't he?

His paintings were scattered throughout the house, huge canvases, many of them filled with images of Hannah. Her favorites, though, were the oils he had done of his wolf brothers. Painting from memory, he had captured them in poses that only one who had lived among them would ever see. There was one of Whitey and his wife playing in a mountain stream, one of them nuzzling each other underneath a full moon while the rest of the pack slept nearby, one of Whitey's wife mourning his death. Her grief was so real Hannah could feel it.

His newest one was of Hannah beside the campfire while a wolf-like figure watched from the shadows. Sensuality leapt from the painting. Looking and remembering, Hannah grew hot.

"Do you like it?" Startled, she whirled to face Hunter. His bold gaze raked her, and he smiled. "I can see that you do."

"The painting is unbelievable."

"So was what I saw from the woods that night. It took every ounce of restraint I had to keep from ravishing you that evening."

"What held you back?"

"Caution. I didn't want to scare you away."

"I had many feelings for you. Fear was not one of them."

"I know that now."

Their eyes locked, and she reached for the top button of her blouse. It slid to the floor and Hunter bent over to take one turgid nipple into his mouth. She leaned against the wall while waves of sensation washed over her. She cupped her breasts and offered them up to him like a feast before gods.

For a small eternity he teased her nipples with tongue and teeth. Then drawing her deep into his mouth, he began to suckle. She went limp with pleasure and would have slid to the floor if he hadn't scooped her up.

He laid her on the hooked wool rug beside the hearth. Reflections from the flames licked over her skin as he stripped off her jeans. Hunter followed the path of firelight with his tongue, found the seat of her passion and plundered there. She spiraled upward, then came crashing back down and shattered into a million pieces.

Tangling her hands in his hair so she could hold him close, she whispered, "This…yes, only this."

He was all she needed, all she wanted. He was sun and wind and stars, moon and rain and comets. He was her universe.

Kneeling over her, he cupped her breasts, then ran his hands over the length of her body, softly, ever so softly. Though he didn't say the words, it felt like love.

"I want you in me," she whispered. "Now."

She opened herself to him, heart, body and soul. Cradling her hips he buried himself deep, and though she didn't say the words, she gave him love.

With firelight flickering over them they explored each other's bodies until they were both sweat-slickened and heaving. And when the flames began to burn low, he lifted his head and shouted his completion to the moon just showing over the windowsill.

A river of passion flooded her, and she wanted to hold it inside forever. She didn't want to move. Not ever.

"Hunter," she whispered, then drew him down and buried her face in his solid wall of chest. She inhaled his scent and tasted the salty dampness of his skin.

Needing no words, he rolled them to their sides and began to caress her back—long, soft strokes that felt like heaven. Hannah closed her eyes and gave herself up to tenderness.

The phone jarred them awake. She and Hunter were still cuddled on the rug in front of the hearth. She eased herself reluctantly out of his embrace.

"I'll get it," she said, though there was absolutely no possibility that he would.

For one thing, as far as the outside world was concerned, Hunter Wolfe did not exist. For another, he hated the telephone. He called it a loud, intrusive, disruptive nuisance.

Mostly, Hannah agreed. She called it a necessary evil.

She padded across the den and picked up the phone. It was her editor.

"Am I calling you too early, Hannah?"

"No. I'm an early riser." Usually. Since Hunter had come into her life, she kept all kinds of bizarre hours, up sometimes until 3:00 a.m. cavorting under the light of a full moon, and sleeping till noon.

God, she was getting spoiled. She could easily adapt to a life without clocks.

"I just wanted to tell you this piece on wolves is the best thing you've ever done."

"Thanks, Jack."

"The readers are going to love it. Especially the animal preservationists. God, Hannah, if this story doesn't elicit sympathy for the plight of the wolf, then our readership is made of stone."

"That's what I was hoping to hear."

"What about the wolfman, Hannah?"

She jerked her head toward Hunter as if someone had suddenly crashed through her doorway and pointed a gun at him.

"What? What do you mean, Jack?"

"I noticed you didn't mention one word of him."

Hunter had come to stand beside her, and she could tell by the tenseness in his muscles that he sensed danger.

"No, I didn't. I tried to keep the story tightly focused."

"It would have made a hell of an addition to the story, Hannah, how they raised him and all that."

"I don't agree."

There was a long silence, and then Jack said, "You got pictures of him, didn't you?"

"When I took that fall, I lost all the film in the camera, plus one other roll."

It wasn't a lie. What she didn't tell him was that she still had some earlier shots of Hunter, some of them superb.

Jack got quiet on his end of the line, and Hannah shifted from one foot to the other. Hunter drew her back against his chest and leaned down to whisper, "Do you want me to take care of him for you?"

She covered the receiver with her hand and whispered, "How?"

"I can scare him to death."

"Thanks, but I can, too." She grinned at Hunter, then turned her attention back to her editor. "Jack, if you're not happy with this story, I can take it somewhere else."

"No...no...I'm happy, Hannah. It's a great story... fabulous."

"You're sure?"

"Positive. Look, sorry I called so early. Go back to bed, and when you're ready for another assignment, just give me a call, okay? There's a story in Tahiti I'd like to talk to you about."

After she'd hung up, Hunter sat on the sofa and pulled her onto his lap.

"He wanted pictures of me, didn't he?"

"Yes, but I told him no."

He retreated into a deep and lonely silence that scared Hannah. Where had he gone? Back to Denali where the winter snows were piled higher than her head and the daylight hours were so short the land was caught in a net of perpetual night?

"You should do a story on me, Hannah."

"No! I won't exploit you. I will *never* exploit you."

Silence fell over him again, and Hannah got cold with fear.

"It's almost time for me to go," he said.

What was there to say? Don't go? Please stay?

When she didn't say anything, Hunter added, "When I make myself known, the press will hound me. I want you to do a story on me, Hannah."

"I can't...."

"You can. And if you don't, you're putting your career in jeopardy."

"Maybe with Jack, but I have other sources for my stories."

"Think about it...I give you an exclusive and I'm not only spared the hassle of dealing with a baying pack of hounds, I'm assured of getting a balanced interview from a thoughtful, intelligent woman who *really* likes me." He grinned at her.

"How do you know I really like you?"

"I have my ways." His *ways* were already stirring to life.

"You certainly do."

When he twisted her around so she was straddling him, she was more than happy for a respite from the disturbing conversation. The thought of his leaving terrified her.

Although it was not like Hannah to retreat from a problem, she secretly hoped Hunter wouldn't bring up the subject of leaving again. She knew she was being selfish and unreasonable, but still, she wanted just a few more days cocooned with him. A few more days to prepare for the inevitable.

Was that too much to ask?

The greatest thing about Hannah's place—besides Hannah herself—was the five-hundred-acre forest. When he was disturbed he always sought solace there.

He stood on the bluff overlooking the river thinking of his future. The prospect of leaving her and making his way in the world shouldn't have scared him, but it did. Fighting for his life in a frozen land filled with peril had frightened him less than facing an uncertain future in a society largely unknown to him.

Hannah was still reluctant to do an exclusive interview. She still protested that she would never use him, never exploit him.

He had known that from the beginning. Instinctively. Otherwise he would never have left Denali. He would have taken his chances with the team sent in to capture him.

He had told her that, but to no avail. Still she resisted. How could he convince her?

Hannah didn't hear the door. She didn't hear footsteps. She didn't hear a sound, but suddenly she *knew* Hunter was in the room.

She tingled all over with awareness.

She turned from her computer to smile at him. "Hunter...I didn't hear you."

"Good. I haven't lost the skill of silence."

"No, you haven't." She didn't miss the note of nostalgia in his voice. Did she hear *longing,* as well?

"You miss Denali, don't you?"

"Yes."

Though she tried not to take his answer personally, pain sliced her heart.

Oh, God, if she didn't get a hold of herself, she was going to be in terrible trouble.

"If I said I'm sorry I took you out of there, I'd be lying. I'm not sorry."

He strode across the room and cupped her face. "Neither am I. I want you to know that, Hannah."

"All right."

"I want you really to understand...I have no regrets...only gratitude." He pulled her close and held her so tightly she almost lost her breath. "I don't know what would have happened to me if you hadn't come along. I will always be grateful to you, Hannah."

Gratitude wasn't all she wanted from him, but it would do. It would have to do, for how could she say all that was in her heart? How could she say I love you without putting a cage around him? The timing was wrong. He had to be free to reclaim his birthright. He had to go into the world unfettered.

Love should be a choice, not a chain.

"I understand," she said. Nothing more.

"I need to talk to you."

"Here or outside?"

Hunter loved it that she knew him so well. Certainly he would have preferred the outdoors, for even though he had been in Mississippi for months now, he still sometimes felt stifled inside.

But winter had come to the South with a vengeance...or as much of a vengeance as it ever did. Overnight the temperature had dropped twenty degrees. He wouldn't expose Hannah to the elements.

"Let's sit by the window," he said, and she laughed.

"Even when you're not outdoors you want to see the outdoors. I should tear out all the windows and put in bigger ones. I should build a few glass walls."

It was the first reference she had made to any kind of future with him. Hunter filed her words away. He would think about them another time.

Right now he had to stay focused. One thing at a time.

That was how he had survived and eventually conquered the wilderness, and that's how he would survive and conquer this new world.

Until then....

He studied Hannah's profile, the high cheekbones and-beautifully sculpted jaw, the lush lips and wide green eyes. Desire pulsed through him, fierce and insistent. With this woman it was always that way.

He could spend almost every waking moment buried in her, and still it would not be enough. A hundred years would not be enough. A thousand.

Hunter reined in his libido. He had things to say, things to do. The future wouldn't wait forever.

"The first thing I need to do is contact my relatives."

She sucked in a sharp breath. That was the only sign of her turmoil.

"Then I'll need to fly to New York," he added. "I'm sure there will be legal tangles."

"I can help you make those arrangements." Her smile was bittersweet. "I know how you hate the telephone."

"I can't do this without you, Hannah."

"You can, of course, but I think I can set things up and smooth the way with a few calls."

"I'm not talking about a few calls. I want you to go with me...if you can."

"Of course I can. But are you sure?"

"I want you at my side all the way. And after I've scared everybody witless by coming back from the dead, I need you to tell the story of my survival to the world." He captured her hands...and her eyes. "Will you please do that for me, Hannah?"

The battle she waged showed on her face. There were several tactics he might have used to win her over quickly, but he waited. He wanted her with him all the way, but he wanted her to *choose* to come.

"If I say no?"

"I will understand. I'll go to New York and take care of business...just like Elvis."

She laughed so long and hard she had to wipe tears from her eyes. It took someone very close to her to see that they weren't all tears of mirth.

"Good lord, you never cease to amaze me. What all have you been watching on television?"

"I'll never tell. Why don't I show you, instead?"

The future could wait, but he couldn't, not another minute, not another second. He gave her a hooded look and clothes flew every which way. Then he scooped her off the sofa and positioned her on the floor.

As he thrust home she shouted, "Yes, yes, yes."

"Is that an answer or a commentary?"

"An answer...don't talk, Hunter...please, please, please."

Chapter Thirty-Five

February 14, 2002

I feel like a queen. Here we are in Tahiti! Another surprise from Michael.

He hadn't said a word about going anywhere for Valentine's Day. But last Tuesday I woke up with this big bulge under my pillow. It turned out to be plane tickets to Tahiti along with a beautiful note from my darling husband.

"My precious one," it said, "I want to spend the most romantic day of the year in another tropical paradise with the most wonderful wife in the universe. All my love forever, Michael...P.S. Pack that sexy red gown and those red high-heeled shoes."

At breakfast I said, "Michael, you keep giving me these marvelous trips and all I'm giving you is a box of chocolates."

He laughed and said, "You give me much, much more, darling."

"But the trips are so expensive."

"I'm more than getting my money's worth. In fact, I think I'll collect right now."

And he did, right there on the kitchen floor. Oh God, this is the most wonderful man on earth. I can't believe I almost lost him.

I know, I know...I shouldn't dwell in the past. And I don't. Not really. Every now and then, though, I startle awake in the middle of the night and reach to the other side of the bed to see if Michael's still there.

I wish I would quit that. The last time it happened (Sunday night after we'd sat up till one watching a particularly scary movie), he said, "Anne, you've got to quit doing this."

"This is the first time in a long time," I told him, and he said, "I hope it's your last."

I guess that's the closest we've been to having a quarrel since he came out of the coma. I take that as a very good sign. In fact, I've slept soundly ever since. Maybe I won't regress.

It's not that I want to forget what happened. I don't. Remembering how I almost lost him has given me a keen appreciation of each moment. I mentally catalog each detail of our day, no matter how mundane.

I can look at the tops of daffodils pushing up through the earth and remember walking through the gardens of Belle Rose holding hands with Michael. I can hear a mocking bird welcoming the day and remember my husband bending over me with a gleam in his eyes and a smile on his dear face. I can see a sunset and remember standing on the white sands of Waikiki embracing my beloved.

He's asleep on a hammock swing just outside our beachfront cottage (another one! I'm getting spoiled by this). I'm going to join him as soon as I finish writing in my diary.

Emily's blooming in her pregnancy. She and Jake are staying at Belle Rose while we're in Tahiti. They both wanted to spend Valentine's Day there. I understand why. It's a house made for love, truly romantic.

Daniel is still high after the concert tour with Skylar. She introduced him at the end of every concert, made him get up on the stage so she could sing the last song for him. The audience loved it, he said, and so did he. Skylar's getting ready to do another music video. When she told me, "This one is going to be a little bit tamer," Daniel chimed in on the extension and said, "I hope not. I'm counting on you to keep the excitement high in this marriage."

They are wonderful together...Jake and Emily, Daniel and Skylar.

It's Hannah I worry about. She and Hunter are in New York now...Ithaca. She flew them up in her plane so they could avoid some of the crowds.

"Things are going smoothly for Hunter," she told us right before we left Belle Rose. (Was it only two days ago?)

"Tell us everything," I said.

"His cousin George couldn't be nicer. When no trace of Hunter was found after seven years, of course he was declared legally dead and George inherited everything. By law he doesn't have to give Hunter a penny. Fortunately, he's a kind-hearted, generous man."

"He's going to give everything back?"

"Not the money he spent on taxes and upkeep of the Wolfe mansion, of course, but the bulk of the estate...yes. Hunter will never have to worry about making a living."

"That's great," I said, but Michael told her, "A man needs to feel useful, Hannah."

"We're working on that, Dad. I'll let you know in a few days. Meantime, we'll be here until the courts reverse his legally dead status."

Naturally, I'm delighted that Hunter is adjusting so well after twenty years in the wilderness, but my main concern is Hannah. When I asked her, "How are you?" she said, "I'm fine, Mom." But that didn't tell me a thing.

Michael says I worry too much about my children, that we did a good job with their upbringing and now we should sit back and watch them fly. I know, I know. He's right.

That's what I'm trying to do. It's easier now that Michael is back. He's not only my lover and my best friend, my rock and my safe port in a storm; he's also the best time I've ever had. Lord, the way we laugh and carry on you'd think we were teenagers instead of fifty-something.

Last night while we lay in our hammock watching the stars I said, "Darling, I love being in this pink cocoon with you. Just the two of us. Do you think we can keep it this way?" And he said, "Always, my precious. Always."

Chapter Thirty-Six

The Wolfe mansion was on a twenty-acre wooded estate that overlooked Cayuga Lake. Hannah was staying in one of the guest suites in the east wing. And that's exactly how she felt…like a guest.

She'd seen Hunter every day, of course…to take care of business, a phrase he had adopted from Elvis. Except for their many business outings and the meals they'd shared, she'd had no contact with him. He didn't come to her at night, he didn't come in the early morning, he didn't suddenly appear during the daylight hours while she was busy tapping away at her computer.

She missed him so much her teeth hurt. Every bone in her body ached for him.

This separation was a good thing, she kept telling herself. It meant she'd done her job well. It meant that Hunter was adjusting to his new circumstances without any problems.

It meant he could resume his life, and she could resume hers.

But, oh, she missed her wolfman. She missed the totally uninhibited man who expressed his every emotion whenever it occurred. She missed the almost-savage who heeded the call of the wild, the pull of the moon.

The Hunter she knew and loved was a force of nature. Had she gone too far with his education? Had she tamed him too much?

She switched off her computer. There was no use trying to work while her mind wandered. Besides, it was time to dress. George was giving a reception in the Wolfe mansion to introduce Hunter to his friends.

Hannah switched on the TV, as much for company as to hear the evening news. Funny how an independent woman could get so used to having someone else around that silence felt lonely.

She was in panties and garter belt when the news broadcast caught her attention.

"Today Hunter Wolfe petitioned the courts of New York to declare him legally alive. Wolfe claims to be the son of Conan and Margaret Wolfe, who died nearly twenty years ago when their plane crashed into a remote region of Denali. No trace was ever found of their nine-year-old son, Hunter. He was presumed dead…until today.

"What happened during those twenty years? Where was he?"

Film of Hunter and Hannah leaving the courtroom flashed on the screen. Reporters swarmed around him, shoving microphones in his face as the voice-over continued.

"Wolfe declined comment and all interviews. More on the mysterious reappearance of the Wolfe heir tonight at…"

The shrill ringing of Hannah's cell phone drowned out his last words. She had barely said hello, when Jack shouted, "I thought you told me he was dead."

"I did."

"Obviously you lied...God, Hannah...I'm hoping you can give me a very good reason for robbing me of the biggest story this magazine has ever had."

"It's personal, Jack."

"*Personal?* Is that all you have to say?"

"Yes, that's all I have to say."

"Then you know what I have to say, don't you?"

"Yes, Jack."

"God, Hannah...you're the best damned photojournalist I've ever worked with...you don't leave me any choice."

"I understand. If I were in your shoes I'd fire me, too."

"Dammit, Hannah, how am I ever going to explain this to my board...you were *right there,* and this magazine has diddley on Hunter Wolfe."

Hannah didn't see Hunter until she felt the phone being lifted out of her hand.

"Jack...this is Hunter Wolfe...that's right...I'm the wolfman...I'm giving an exclusive interview to Hannah...I thought so...I'll tell her."

He ended the connection, then tossed the phone onto a bedside table.

"Jack says to tell you he's sorry. He looks forward to getting your story."

"How dare you!" Hannah stomped to the window and glared at the lake, then whirled around with her hands on her hips and her chin outthrust. "I've been taking care of myself for years. I don't need or want you or anybody else to do it for me."

"You agreed to do the interview."

"I did not."

"I recall it vividly. You said, *yes, yes, yes.*"

"I was talking about coming to New York with you...wipe that wicked grin off your face. I *will not* exploit you, and I *will not* be sidetracked by you."

She was lying, of course. His eyes gleamed silvery with passion, and her body responded like a seasoned racehorse. To make matters worse, she was standing around in next to nothing with nowhere to hide.

Not that she would. She'd be darned if she would retreat. Hunter might intimidate many people, she was not one of them, regardless of his size.

When he saw where her treacherous eyes had strayed, he grinned even more.

"Don't think you can ignore me for days, and them come in here and I'll fall like a ripe plum."

"I was thinking more of peaches. You taste like ripe peaches, Hannah."

He was irresistible...almost. Languid with desire, Hannah moved in slow motion to get a robe.

"The party will be starting soon. You don't want to be late."

"I haven't lived with a clock for twenty years. I don't plan to start now."

"Well, I do. George has been extremely nice. He deserves every courtesy."

"Hannah...come here."

Their eyes locked and held. Suddenly they rushed into each other's arms. Hunter buried his face in her hair and inhaled.

"I've missed you, Hannah."

"I know. I've missed you, too."

His fingertips traced the line of her jaw, then moved softly into the neck of her robe. How could he tell her all he was feeling? How could he convey his confusion, his uncertainty?

He couldn't. It was that simple. He couldn't keep using Hannah to keep the rest of the world at bay. He couldn't continue to use her as a sweet hot shield against reality.

He had to find his own way. Until then...

He pulled back and smiled down at her. "You're not going to throw me to the wolves again, are you?"

"You did all right the first time."

"Think how many people you will help with a story of my survival. Think of all the young readers who might someday find themselves lost in the woods."

"You're shameless."

"I know."

"I took a noble savage and turned him into a shark."

"You'll do the story, won't you? You're the only one I trust." Watching the play of emotions on her face, he knew the exact moment when she changed her mind.

She nodded yes, then said, "I liked you better when you were running around in a bearskin."

He held her a moment longer, tethered to sanity by her soft fragrant skin.

"So did I." He left quickly, while he still could.

Hannah stood near the French doors watching Hunter charm the crowds that followed him. From the moment he'd walked into the room, he'd been surrounded. She'd have had a hard time getting close even if she wanted to.

Give him room to breathe, she kept telling herself. *Give him space.* And then, *Give him freedom.*

If she were seeing him for the first time she would not have guessed that he had never attended a cocktail party, let alone been the life of one. He was easily the most self-confident man in the room. Or so it seemed.

Only when she looked closely did she see the haunted look in his eyes. He missed Denali. More than missed it. A part of him seemed to be dying without it. What had she done?

"Hannah...." George came up beside her holding two glasses of wine. He was twenty years older than Hunter, a distinguished man with graying hair at his temples and wire-rimmed glasses. He had an air of quiet reserve and sincerity that had drawn Hannah to him immediately.

"Drink?" he asked.

"Yes, thank you."

"He's quite a success, isn't he?" He nodded toward his cousin. "Thanks to you."

"I can't take much credit. He's brilliant, and obviously very adaptable."

George shook his head. "I still can't believe he's alive, after all these years. He doesn't talk much about what happened except to say he learned a lot about survival." He laughed. "I guess I'll have to wait and read your story."

"He told you I was doing a story?"

"Yes, this morning at breakfast."

Hours before she'd agreed. Hannah felt a secret flash of pride at his self-confidence. For that, at least, she liked to think that she deserved some of the credit.

"I want you to know that Sarah and I really appreciate everything you've done for Hunter."

George's wife smiled at her from across the room. She looked like a young, blond Jackie Kennedy, tall and regal, the perfect hostess for her successful investment banker husband. She was also a successful career woman in her own right, a stockbroker, which in part accounted for the excellent state of Hunter's bank account.

"It has been the most unforgettable experience of my life. To say I've enjoyed it would be an understatement."

Heat flushed her face as memories flooded her. She hoped George didn't notice.

"He told me this morning that he wants Sarah and me to keep the house, that he has no intention of living here. I tried to decline, but he insisted."

Hannah's heart jumped into her throat. If not here, then where? Mississippi? Did she dare hope?

"He didn't say what his plans are," George added. "I thought you might know."

"I don't know where he plans to live. All I know is that he has a private showing in the Clifford Gallery in New York next month."

"I told him he always has a home here. So did Sarah. She's become very fond of Hunter."

So had she. More than fond. Hannah was in love with him…and it was tearing her to pieces. To tell or not to tell? What if he left because he thought she didn't love him? Or what if he left because she *did,* and it stifled him?

"Will your story be out by then?"

"Yes." Her spirits lifted. All those interviews. She'd have to be with him a while longer.

"That ought to jump-start his career as an artist…if that's what he wants."

Hannah watched Hunter across the room. His natural charm and easy manner conveyed nothing of his real feelings. Who knew what Hunter wanted?

Chapter Thirty-Seven

Hunter was surrounded by a pack of yapping females with painted faces, and he wanted to run. Or else bare his teeth, growl at them and scare them away.

The only thing that kept him from embarrassing his cousin George was Hannah. She was across the room from him, a cool oasis in a desert of confusion. Dressed simply in black, she stood apart and above the other women. She needed no ornamentation. Her face was enough.

She was stunning. Her beauty had always appealed to him, but until now he'd had no basis of comparing her with other women. She was head and shoulders above.

And she was the only thing that kept him sane. Wherever he moved, he kept her in sight.

"Did you learn to howl?"

The inane question, prompted no doubt by tonight's television broadcast, was put to him by a silly woman with too much makeup. Hunter started to ignore the remark, then changed his mind.

"Yes, I like to spend my free time that way."

That sent her off at a fast trot. People stopped to chat as he worked his way toward Hannah. Out of the corner of his eye he saw a handsome young man with an insincere smile join Hannah, then lean too close—much, much too close. The man said something that made her laugh.

Hunter wanted to take him by the scruff of the neck and throw him into the lake.

"Excuse me, please," he said, then stalked off to claim his mate. She was his. Let the man who challenged him beware. He would fight to the death for her.

As he passed a silly Greek statue that he didn't remember from his childhood, two women started toward him, took one look at his face and scurried away. That gave Hunter pause.

He must look every inch the savage. What was he thinking? He was at a cocktail party in Ithaca, not the wilderness of Denali.

The rules here were different. Here you didn't make a woman yours simply by mounting her then taking her to a place where she would be safe from her natural enemies. Here the courtships sometimes took years, as in the case of George and Sarah. Then you had to have other people pronounce your union legal, with a document as further proof of your commitment.

The next level of complication arose in the matter of where you lived. Safety wasn't enough. Judging by the way Sarah and George had refurbished the Wolfe mansion, ostentation and excess seemed to be the guiding principles.

The whole idea repelled Hunter. People made elaborate, debt-ridden prisons for themselves, then fortified themselves with alcohol and told themselves that their lives were good.

Hunter could never live that way. He'd known that almost from the moment he'd arrived in Ithaca to reclaim his birthright. Giving the house to George had not been a sacrifice; it had been a relief.

But what of Hannah? She hadn't spent the last twenty years in a wilderness. She was accustomed to the elaborate rituals Hunter found so repressive.

He slowed his pace and reined in his urge to do bodily harm. By the time he reached Hannah and her admirer, he gave every impression of being relaxed. Or so he hoped.

"Hello, Hannah."

The smile that had started in her eyes wavered. She turned quickly to the man beside her and said, "Chester, will you please excuse us for a moment?"

"Certainly."

When the man bent over to kiss Hannah's hand, Hunter felt his hackles rising again. There's no telling what he would have done if the other man hadn't left.

"Follow me, Hunter."

"Does my anger show?"

"That...among other things."

They moved swiftly toward the French doors and outside into the garden. A crescent moon glowed in sharp relief to a black velvet sky. Here and there a star shone through the branches of winter-naked trees.

They skirted a wrought-iron table and chairs, then hurried across the lawn, through the gate in the brick wall and down the long dark path. They didn't stop until they reached a secluded grove at the edge of the lake. No chattering people. No nosey questions. No prying eyes. Just Hannah and the safe canopy of trees with the water sparkling beyond.

At last Hunter felt as if he could breathe. He inhaled the cold, sharp air.

"Thank you, Hannah."

"You're welcome."

"You've rescued me once more."

"Anytime." She wrapped her arms around herself, shivering.

"You shouldn't have come out here without a coat." Hunter pulled off his tuxedo jacket and wrapped it around her. She turned the collar up around her face and snuggled inside.

"You'll freeze," she said, and he laughed.

"In Denali this kind of weather would be considered a warm spell."

"I almost forgot...."

She broke off and gazed across the water. What was she thinking? Was she remembering the quiet woods by the Mississippi? The long, lazy days when they had laughed often and loved at will?

Was she remembering their first mating beside the river? The way she had curled into him and slept on the forest floor? The raw, wild passion? The unbridled pleasure?

"Hannah?"

He moved close behind her and lifted a strand of dark hair that caressed her cheek. When she turned he saw the dampness of unshed tears in her eyes.

"Hunter...make love to me."

Without a word he positioned her on the carpet of fragrant fallen cedar leaves. When he entered her, his world righted. Rules vanished, convention disappeared and time faded. There was only the moment...and this...this incredible joining that felt like the merging of two rivers.

Hunter flowed with the tides of pleasure, rode the currents of passion. And when the waves of completion crashed over him, he lifted his head and howled his pleasure to the thin silver moon.

Then he turned Hannah in his arms and lay with her there among the crushed cedar boughs, shielding her against the cold. Neither of them talked. Neither of them tried to explain what had happened and why. They merely accepted the inevitable.

It had always been that way between them.

They stayed cocooned in their soft afterglow until he felt a shiver run through her.

"You're cold," he said.

"A little."

"We'll go inside the back way."

"What about the party?"

"You don't have to go back...unless you want to."

"I don't."

"Good. I'll brush the forest debris off myself, then go back and make my excuses to George."

"Will you come to me afterward?"

"I don't want to use you, Hannah."

"I don't feel used."

He might have asked, "How do you feel? *What* do you feel?" But the moment passed, and he discovered that it was too soon for him to know. Right now, he had everything he could handle.

"I've missed you, Hunter," she said, mistaking his silence for refusal.

"I'll be there, Hannah," he said, and she nodded.

They didn't talk going back. He led her through a rear gate and up the back stairs. At her room he kissed her once, hard, then hurried off to play the civilized man.

Hannah undressed in the dark then lay down on her bed. Suddenly she felt overwhelmed. Since they had left Mississippi so much had happened so quickly.

Thoughts ran squirrel-like around her mind, but she pushed them firmly away. She couldn't deal with one more important issue.

She would rest a moment then get up and take a shower, wash the bits and pieces of cedar out of her hair. Hunter wouldn't be back for another hour. Maybe even two.

She heard the click of the lock, then felt his weight on the bed.

"Hunter?" She heard the rustle of his clothes, then the muted thump as they hit the floor. "I didn't expect you back so soon. What about the party?"

"I told George and Sarah good-night. The rest of them don't matter."

Sensations ripped through her as he circled her nipples with his fingertips.

"Only this matters," he said. "Only this."

And then he lifted her hips and drove inside. Pleasure splintered through her, and she covered her mouth to stifle her cry.

"Don't." Hunter moved her hand away. "This house is huge and these walls are thick. No one will hear…except me." He executed a maneuver that brought out another shattered cry.

"I love the sounds you make," he said, and then drove her to such a frenzy that she set new records in love cries.

It had been so long. So long.

She couldn't get enough of him. Time and again he spun her toward the stars then brought her crashing back to the earth. And still she wanted him…as he wanted her.

In each other they could deny the truth, hold back time. Reason had no reign in their bedroom. Reality had no meaning. The only thing that mattered was the two of them—together.

Sweat slicked their bodies as they heaved against each other. Hunter rolled onto his back, taking her with him. Lifting her hair off her hot neck, she began a wild ride that shattered them both.

She slumped against him, limp, and he stroked her back in a slow, smooth motion.

"Hunter...."

"Shhh...don't talk."

"Will you stay?"

"Yes."

"Good."

That was the last thing she remembered until she woke up sometime before dawn. His eyes gleamed silver as his hands continued their delicious stroking.

"That's what woke me?" she murmured.

"Yes. That's what." He pressed closer. "And this...."

She slid under the covers and took him in her mouth...and the magic started all over again.

Under the guise of "being interviewed," Hunter spent every moment of the next two weeks in her room.

"This is the only interview I've ever conducted naked," she told him.

"Good."

"I have to get down to the business at hand or I'll never get the story written."

"You already know the story."

"Most of it. There are some gaps."

Hannah started to put on her robe, but when he said, "Don't," she let it slide to the floor.

"I like you without clothes."

"I've discovered I like not wearing them. There's a certain freedom...."

She couldn't quite explain it, but he knew. Smiling, he said, "Yes."

"I'm going to tape you now, okay?" He nodded. "After your parents' plane crashed and you realized there was faint hope of rescue, how did you feel?"

"At first, trapped, then free and trapped at the same time, and later...merely free."

Could she make that progression clear to her readers? She hoped so.

"Tell me about your cave drawings...everything."

"Initially, I used them merely as a way to keep track of the days. After months of hearing nothing but the sound of my own voice, I wrote a few things—my name, the date of the plane crash, the names I had given my wolf friends."

Suddenly he walked to the window where he stood looking out. Hannah waited. She'd seen the longing that came into his face the minute he mentioned the wolves.

When he turned back to her, he said, "They were family to me."

I understand, she wanted to tell him, and yet she didn't. Not really. How could she? Only someone who had experienced the isolation, the terror, the awe of living alone in the wilderness for twenty years could possibly understand.

He sat down again on the floor and began to talk. He told her of killing his first bear, of making winter clothes from the skin, of making weapons and learning to treat his wounds. And he told her of the vast silence that gradually stole all his verbal skills except the few he kept alive...the names of his constant companions.

As she listened, she knew what she would write: the story of a man who came to think of himself as a wolf.

Chapter Thirty-Eight

The entire Westmoreland family as well as Clarice gathered in New York for Hunter's showing at the Clifford Gallery. It would be Hannah's first time seeing Hunter in two weeks, two very long weeks. During that time he'd been in Ithaca while she'd been in Mississippi gearing up for another assignment, this time in South America. Jack wanted her to do a story on the alarming disappearance of the rain forest.

"That first installment you did on Hunter Wolfe was a sensation," he'd told her when he called about the rain-forest assignment. "Readers are chomping at the bit for the second installment. Circulation doubled. I'm proud of you, Hannah."

She was proud of herself, but not because of increased circulation. The magazine had received more letters from that story than any they'd ever done. "Journalism with heart," a reader from New Jersey called her piece. "I used a whole box of tissues when I read Hannah Westmoreland's story,'' another from Canada wrote. ''What we need is more Hannah Westmorelands in the media. Her compassionate telling of Hunter Wolfe's story gives journalists a much-needed boost in reputation.''

Several readers had written, ''I can't wait to see how the story ends.''

Neither could she.

She hadn't seen Hunter since the publication of the first installment. What would be his reaction to her story? To her?

''You look pensive, Hannah.'' Her mother had joined her in the lobby of the Algonquin where she was waiting for her cab. ''I'm worried about you.''

''Quit worrying, Mom. Just keep having fun with Dad. I can take care of myself.''

''I didn't say you couldn't. I just know that you haven't been yourself since this whole business with Hunter started.''

''You're right. I haven't. It's high time I got back on track.''

''What track is that, Hannah?''

Hannah studied her Mom for a moment before answering. ''You should hang out a shingle.''

Anne laughed. ''That's what your father says.'' She reached for her daughter's hand. ''Have you told him what you want?''

''If you're talking about Hunter, forget it.''

''Of course, I'm talking about Hunter. Who else? You've finally met your match, Hannah, and I say it's about damned time.''

''Mom!'' She had never heard her mother use that word, or any strong language, for that matter. It was so totally out of character, Hannah laughed.

"I've never known you to be timid," Anne said.

"That stings." She considered herself to be bold and courageous, but her mother's words had the ring of truth, and Hannah never ran from the truth. Except where love was involved. In matters of the heart, she was out of her element. An elephant tromping on petunias.

"Hannah, I've never met a man who can read minds. Except maybe your father. When you love someone you have to tell him what you want in order for him to give it to you."

"That's easy for you to say."

"I know, but not everybody is lucky enough to have a Michael. The thing is, men want to give you what you want."

"Hunter's different."

"He's a man, isn't he?"

"He's *all* man."

"I rest my case."

The crowd that filled the gallery amazed Hunter, though he shouldn't have been surprised, not after Hannah's story. How many of them had come to see his art and how many had come to gape at him?

He wasn't long finding out. A woman wearing enough fur to outfit a grizzly approached him.

"Mr. Wolfe? This is the most stunning collection I've seen in years."

"Thank you...."

"Jenny Vanlandingham. Call me Jenny. Everybody does."

She didn't look like the kind of woman you'd be on familiar terms with after two years, let alone two minutes.

"I'm glad you like my work."

"*Like* it? My dear boy, I'm going to break the bank

buying it." She tapped him on the arm with her program. "Tell me, who is the exquisite woman?"

"Hannah Westmoreland." He was glad Hannah wanted people to know.

"The woman who wrote that fabulous story!"

"The same."

Jenny turned to look at the one of Hannah on their tumbled bed. It bore a Not For Sale tag.

"Extraordinary...that painting in particular...she must be very special to you."

Hunter had not thought about his relationship with Hannah in those terms. She was the one he had chosen. Until recently it had been that simple.

He gazed across the crowd just as she came through the door. She wore a stunning red dress...and an incomparable face. Someone in the crowd recognized her as the subject of most of his art collection and started applauding.

Hannah acknowledged the applause with a smile and a nod. The crowd parted as she made her way toward Hunter.

"She's very special," he told Jenny Vanlandingham.

"Better steal a private moment with her while you can."

Hannah had not had to search the room for Hunter. She'd felt the magnetic pull of his eyes the minute she walked in the door.

Now, as she approached, she felt his body heat, as well. She was glad her dress was strapless, glad she'd checked her velvet wrap at the door. Even so, she felt as if she'd stepped into the middle of an inferno.

"Hunter." He took her hand, and she felt the jolt all the way to her toes. "You're a huge hit."

"So are you...if that stampede coming this way is any indication."

She glanced over her shoulder and winced. She'd never expected such a reaction.

"Brace yourself," she told him.

"Not yet."

He took her by the arm and whisked her up a narrow staircase and into a small room with two stuffed chairs and a sturdy table that held a coffeepot and a tray of mugs. He closed the door, then pushed a chair against it.

"That should keep them at bay," he said.

"This is your show. We can't stay here."

"We can until I do this." He pulled her close and kissed her until they both lost their breath.

She leaned her face against his chest and inhaled the clean outdoor scent of him. Even after all these months it seemed to Hannah that he still wore the scent of the wilderness.

All the things she'd meant to say to him vanished, and in their place stood the simple truth.

"I've missed you," she said.

"And I've missed you." He leaned back and stroked her hair. "Do you know that your hair looks like the pelt of a very fine dark female wolf?"

She smiled at him, but something in his face constricted her throat.

"I want you, Hannah, but if I start now I won't stop till morning."

The idea made her weak-kneed. "I know," she whispered.

"After the show, then?"

"Yes. After the show."

"I'll go down first to deflect some of the attention. You can stay here as long as you like."

"Hiding is not my style."

Hunter laughed. "I know that better than anyone."

He kissed her once more, hard, then strode out the door and closed it behind him. Hannah put her hands over her mouth and sank onto one of the chairs.

Tonight was a turning point for Hunter. He had taken the art world by storm and would soon have them at his feet. Would it hold him? Would she?

Or was the pull of the wilderness too strong?

"What am I going to do?" she whispered.

Muted sounds drifted up the staircase. "Not stay up here and hide, that's for sure."

Hannah took a compact from her evening bag and touched up her face. Then she went downstairs to face the music.

Her brother was the first one she saw. He was standing at the foot of the stairway, his tall, muscular frame blocking the rest of the room from view.

"Well, Sis, you always did have a flair for the dramatic."

She didn't try to hedge. After all, this was Daniel. The two of them had never kept secrets from each other. Until Hunter....

"I thought about hiring a plane to skywrite Hannah Plus Hunter, then I decided the paintings were a dead giveaway."

"Nobody with half a brain will mistake you for a mere artist's model."

"Do you approve?"

He grinned at her. "Do you need my approval?"

"No...but I would like to know what you think."

"I think Hunter's amazingly resourceful, remarkable and clearly talented."

"Anyone reading my story and viewing his paintings could have said that, Daniel. I want to know what you really think."

"I like him."

"But?"

"But what?"

"Don't hedge with me, Daniel. I want to know exactly what you think. Then, of course, I'll do as I darned well please."

He laughed. "Here goes, then. I don't think this is a man who will ever be tamed. Make sure you understand that."

Her brother spoke the truth. She'd known that about Hunter almost from the beginning.

"I'm not the kind of woman who wants a tame man."

"Then go for it." He hugged her, then said, "Let me be your escort for a while. I saw a few barracudas out there."

When she entered the gallery she saw her parents and Clarice talking to Hunter. Skylar was with Jake and Emily standing underneath a giant painting of a white wolf.

"What did the rest of the family say when they saw the paintings?" Hannah asked.

"You know them. They didn't blink an eye. Skylar said she'd never seen you look more beautiful, and Mom agreed."

"And Dad?"

"You know Dad. He said how proud he is of you, then got this look in his eye that meant he'd be talking to Hunter in private."

She had no time to think about that because the press had spotted her. They began to fire questions.

"What is your relationship with Hunter Wolfe?"

"In the last few months I've been his friend, his teacher and his model."

"Are you having an affair?"

"No comment."

"Do you plan to marry him?"

"No comment."

"What are Hunter Wolfe's plans?"

"You'll have to ask him."

"Will he be going back to Mississippi with you?"

"I can't answer that question."

"Were you afraid of him when you first saw him?"

"Never."

"What was your agenda when you brought him out of Denali?"

She held up her hand. "No more questions. This is Hunter's show. I'm merely a guest, just as you are."

All of them left except one aggressive young man who shouldered his way close and said, "What was it like being intimate with a wolfman?"

Daniel turned to Hannah and said, "I'll get Hunter."

She and her brother had worked as a team so long they could practically read each other's minds.

"Okay," she said.

As Daniel stalked off, the reporter struggled for composure. Hannah repressed her laughter.

"What can Hunter Wolfe tell me that you can't?"

"He's not going to *say* anything. It's what he's going to do that you should worry about."

His face turned a sick shade of green, and he quickly vanished into the crowd.

"Did it work?" Daniel asked when he returned.

"It worked." They gave each other high fives. "Let's go and see some art."

Chapter Thirty-Nine

March 28, 2002

I'm sitting here at this lovely antique desk in our suite while Michael sleeps. I lay beside him for a long time watching him sleep before I came in here. Lord, he's so gorgeous in repose. I wish I had Hunter Wolfe's talent. I'd paint him...those incredible cheekbones, that strong square jaw, the wonderful cleft in his chin. And his long black eyelashes...Lord, no wonder our girls are so spectacular.

Emily is positively glowing, and I've never seen Hannah look more beautiful. Those paintings took my breath away. They still do, even now, hours later, just thinking about them.

There's an intimacy in them that is sacred, a passion that is palpable.

Michael felt it too. He didn't say anything, but he

reached for me, and we viewed the rest of the show holding hands.

Then while Michael was talking to Hunter, Clarice told me, "I have to have one of these for my bedroom. If they ring Larry's chimes as much as they do mine, you can start looking for another matron of honor dress."

"You're not thinking of marrying again!"

"Why not? I'm getting too old to live in sin."

"Don't mention age. In my mind we're both still sixteen."

"I was just kidding. I'm going to be young and outrageous forever."

"So am I," I told her, and then as soon as we got back to our hotel I proved it to myself and Michael both.

Afterward, Michael said, "Remember our first time here, Anne?"

"How could I forget?"

He kissed me and said, "Darling, every time is like the first."

Oh, it is. It is. The excitement never wanes with us. So many people don't have what Michael and I do. I can't imagine living without the spontaneous fun, the remarkable passion, the magic.

I hope I never have to. I hope that when our time comes to die, we will look at each other and nod, then hold hands and walk off into the great beyond together.

I think Emily and Daniel have found that kind of love. I believe Hannah has, too, though I'm not sure she fully realizes that.

She left with Hunter tonight. I don't expect her back, though of course, I won't know until morning. And I'll know only what she chooses to tell.

My children have lives of their own, and I do too. Thank God.

Daniel and Skylar and Jake and Emily are flying home tomorrow. Michael and I are staying another two weeks.

When I said, "You're spoiling me," he said, "Call it another honeymoon."

"I've lost count of the number of honeymoons we've had since you woke up."

"Good," he said, and I could tell he was pleased...not only that I had lost count, but that I had mentioned his recent coma as if it were merely something that happened to us. An extraordinary event, to be sure, but no longer terrifying.

He still hasn't talked about it, though, except to say that he heard every word, felt every touch.

"You brought me back, Anne." That's what he tells me at least once a week.

Someday I hope he can tell me what it was like being alone in the dark for so many months. Was he scared? Lonely? Peaceful? Free?

When the time is right, he'll tell me. Until then, I have this...the greatest love of all time.

Chapter Forty

Hunter's room at the St. Moritz overlooked Central Park. The curtains were open and in the wee hours of the morning, while most of the world slept, it was almost like being outside.

Hannah and her wolfman lay on the carpet facing a brilliant sliver of moon and stars so bright they burned holes through the night. As sweat cooled on her body, she shivered and Hunter pulled the spread off the bed to cover her.

She wanted to cuddle close to him and fall asleep, but more than that she wanted to *know* that when she woke up in the morning he would be there. What to say? What to do?

They had reached a turning point. With the success of the show, Hunter had achieved credibility as an artist. There was nothing more she could teach him, nothing more she could do for him.

Except love him.

The thought whispered through her mind, and with it her mother's advice.

Still, Hannah hesitated. Loving Hunter was only part of the equation. He had to love her back.

There was no doubt that he wanted her. Lord, hadn't he proved that over and over?

But he had to *choose* her. That was the important thing. And in order to know whether he would, she had to set him free.

She shifted so she could see his face. "Hunter, I've taken an assignment in South America."

"When do you leave?"

"In a few days."

"For how long?"

"As long as the story takes. I'll probably be down there a month."

He didn't say anything for a long while, but gazed out the window with a faraway look in his eyes.

"I'll miss you," he finally said.

"I'll miss you, too."

He started stroking her arms in the slow, soft movements she loved so well. How easy it would be to close her eyes and drift away on a sea of contentment.

"Hunter...what will you do?"

"I don't know, Hannah...I know some things I'm not going to do."

"Such as..."

"Live in New York. George and Sarah want me to stay with them in Ithaca, but I'm not going to do that. It's no longer home to me."

Did that mean he was going back to Alaska? Was it possible he would stay in Mississippi?

"Mississippi can be your home...if you choose." He was quiet. "Could you live there, Hunter?"

He lifted himself on his elbow, and in the moonlight he looked almost as he had when she'd first seen him watching her from the deep snowy woods.

"Could you live in Denali?"

Live how? In a tent? In a house? In a cave? She wasn't ready to ask those questions. She didn't want him to feel tied down, hemmed in, imprisoned by her expectations.

"I don't know," she said.

"Neither do I."

She felt the tension building in him, the heat. When he pressed her back against the fallen coverlet, she wrapped arms and legs around him and welcomed him back, welcomed him to the only home he knew.

They loved each other with fierce passion...and with aching tenderness. They loved until the sun pinked the windowsill. And when they both gave one final ecstatic cry, Hannah knew this would be the last time for a very long time. Perhaps forever.

Hunter held her close for a while without speaking. And then he said, "I'm going back to Denali."

"I know," she whispered.

"I have to...."

"You don't have to explain. I understand." She twisted in his arms. "I'll fly you back in."

"Yes," he said.

There was nothing left to say, nothing left to do. Hannah gathered her things, and when she was dressed she said, "The day after tomorrow. I'll pick you up in Ithaca."

She left quickly without looking back. They had already said goodbye.

The knock on her hotel room door woke Hannah. "Just a minute," she said, then grabbed her robe and opened the door.

Anne came in bearing food—two steaming cups of coffee and a bag of pastries. "Soul food, good for what ails you."

"How do you know what ails me?"

"I can see." Her mother handed her a cup and two packs of sugar. "Talk when you're ready."

"I'm taking him back to Denali."

"Oh, Hannah...."

"I need to go anyway. I want to see the cave paintings and take a few pictures for the next installment of my story. Stop worrying, Mom."

"What? I didn't say anything."

"You didn't have to. I saw that look." Hannah fortified herself with a big bite of pastry. "I'll head to South America as soon as I leave Denali. I'll be so busy the next few weeks I won't have time to think about personal problems."

"In a pig's eye." Hannah laughed, and her mother said, "I mean it, Hannah. When you love someone, he's never far from your mind. After I met Michael I didn't stop thinking about him for two seconds straight."

"You exaggerate."

"Only a little. I thought of him *constantly.* That's what happens when you find *the one.*"

"It's wonderful to see you so happy again. You look twenty years younger."

"Really? I think I've put on five pounds."

"I don't hear Dad complaining."

"He doesn't have time. I keep him occupied."

Anne laughed with her head thrown back and her face shining, and Hannah thought, Only a woman truly loved looks like that.

She envied that. Did Hunter truly love her, or did he

merely want her? With his background, would he ever know the difference? And would it matter to her?

Or would he simply choose to return to the wild?

"Will you join us for lunch before you fly back home?"

"Yes. I'll want to see Dad before I leave."

Hannah finished loading her gear for South America into her plane, then went back into her cottage and pulled open the closet door. Hunter's bearskin clothes and his primitive weapons lay inside.

If she didn't take them, maybe he wouldn't stay. If she did she would be saying to him, "The choice is yours."

She hesitated only a moment before packing them in a duffle bag and taking them out to the plane. Within an hour she was suited up and flying to Ithaca. She wouldn't think about the purpose of her journey. She would only think about weather conditions.

When Hannah walked through the door of the Wolfe mansion something inside Hunter settled down and said, *There now.* It amazed him that she had such power over him...the power to calm as well as excite.

Neither of them said hello. Instead they stared...and sizzled. It started as a slow heat that quickly escalated to a towering inferno.

Hunter reined in his passion.

"Was your flight good?"

"Yes. The weather cooperated. It's supposed to be clear tomorrow, too."

"Good."

He never took his eyes off hers. How could he? He was drowning.

"I brought your bearskins and weapons."

"Thank you...George and Sarah have dinner planned here."

"Fine," she said.

What was she thinking? Was she remembering how they'd slipped out of the party and made love beside the lake?

"Sarah has your room ready."

"I'll go and freshen up, then."

"I'll get your bag."

When he passed by her, he reeled from the nearness. What was he thinking, leaving this woman?

Hannah wore a red strapless gown for dinner. Vanity, she guessed. A last-ditch effort to show Hunter what he would be missing if he stayed in Denali.

Before she chastised herself for stooping to games, she remembered that throughout the animal kingdom preening and strutting are common in the courtship ritual. The idea of courtship was ridiculous, of course. She and Hunter had progressed far, far beyond that point.

But where would they go from here?

Her eyes locked on his, and stayed that way throughout dinner. She ate little and tasted nothing.

Here she was sitting across the table from her entire universe, and she might as well be on another planet.

Hunter paced his room, wrestling with demons. In the hallway the grandfather clock struck midnight. The rest of the house was sleeping. Or were they?

Was Hannah lying in her bed waiting for him? Wanting him as much as he wanted her?

He started toward her room, then made himself turn back. If he went to her tonight, he could never leave her.

And if he didn't leave her, he would always wonder if he should have gone back to Denali.

Taking nothing except the clothes on his back, Hunter hurried out of the house and down to the lake. He stood for a moment with his face uplifted to the glow of the moon, then made a bed of cedar boughs under the trees where he and Hannah had made love.

For once, though, nature did not soothe the savage beast.

Chapter Forty-One

The snows still wrapped Denali in a thick blanket. She banked the plane without looking at Hunter. She was afraid of what she would see in his face.

Instead she concentrated on her landing. "I'm going to try to bring us down in the same spot I used last fall. Is there anything I should know about what the snow does to this particular terrain?"

"It's a natural runway, and you're a good pilot. You'll be fine, Hannah."

After she'd landed, Hunter helped her set up camp. Once again she chose the site she'd used when she first met him. She'd never considered herself superstitious, but wasn't that a good omen? Returning to the scene where she'd first come under his spell?

"Will you stay here tonight, Hunter?"

"No."

"Where will you go?"

"To find the wolves." He touched her face. "I'll see you in the morning, Hannah."

Pride got in the way of common sense. "I can find the cave by myself."

He laughed. "I know you can. I want to show it to you. I want to see your face when you discover it."

"Oh." She felt foolish, but quickly forgave herself. When you loved someone as much as she loved Hunter, you were bound to make a fool of yourself every now and then.

"Do you have everything you need before I go?"

"Yes. I'm fine."

He picked up his primitive weapons and the duffle bag that held his bearskins, then stood studying her. Was he reluctant to leave? She hoped so. She hoped leaving her was the hardest thing he'd ever done.

She held her breath, waiting for him to change his mind, waiting for him to say, "Since you're going to be here a few days, it would be foolish for me not to stay with you."

Instead, he said, "I'll see you later," then disappeared into the woods.

She stood listening to the eerie silence. How could he have vanished so completely, so quickly?

All those months of training to become "civilized" had not destroyed his animal instincts. As she watched the silent woods, something in Hannah exulted.

She jumped at every sound. Hannah snapped on her flashlight and looked at the dial of her watch. Midnight. Would she ever sleep?

All of a sudden the back of her neck prickled. Not from fear but from excitement. Hunter was out there somewhere, nearby.

She lay in her sleeping bag listening for a sound that

would give him away, but all she heard was the soughing of the wind in the trees. Hannah snapped off her light. All she needed was the evidence of her senses.

Smiling, she folded her hands under her cheek and closed her eyes. She was at peace. Her wolfman was keeping watch.

When Hannah saw him the next morning she experienced a sense of dèjá vu. Dressed in bearskins with the snowy mountains as backdrop, he was every inch the wild and free wolfman she'd first seen.

"Hunter?"

"I didn't mean to scare you, Hannah." He came into the clearing smiling.

"You didn't scare me. I didn't expect...." She didn't know what she had expected. "Coffee will be ready in a minute."

"I'm going to miss coffee...among other things."

She held his gaze as long as she could bear. "Did you find your wolf family?"

"Yes."

"How did they react?"

"They were happy to see me. Wouldn't your family be happy to see you after a long absence?"

"Yes, of course...I feel awkward about all this, Hunter. Interviewing you in the Wolfe mansion was easy, but I'm out of my element here, and struggling to understand a relationship that is totally beyond my experience. Or the experience of anyone I've ever known."

"I don't know how to explain it to you. I don't analyze my connection to the wolves, Hannah. I just accept it."

A deep truth settled into her bones: if she didn't accept his loyalties to the wolves she would lose him.

"Let's have coffee, then I'll be ready to see the cave."

* * *

They made the long climb to the cave mostly in silence. Although it had been months since she was there, Hannah recognized most of the landmarks. Still, she was glad Hunter was leading.

She didn't see any signs of the wolves.

"They know I need to do this alone," Hunter said.

"You read my mind."

"Yes."

"Can you always do that?"

"No. Only when you are open to me."

"I'll have to be more careful."

"Why?"

"A woman needs a few secrets."

This sort of camaraderie was easy in the daytime. It was the nights that brought uncertainty and fear.

They topped the last ridge and the entrance to the cave loomed ahead.

"I'll go first." Hunter took a powerful flashlight and turned the beam into the dark interior. "Watch your head."

Hannah ducked in after him and followed a distance of thirty feet on hands and knees. Suddenly the ceiling opened up, and she was standing in an enormous cavern with a thin beam of light coming through a natural skylight twenty feet up.

As her eyes adjusted to the dim light she saw Hunter's weapons neatly stacked in one corner of the cave, a pallet of bearskins and three large utensils that looked as if they had been made from the wreckage of the plane. In the center was a fire pit. She could only guess at the effort it had taken him to create a spark in order to build a fire.

But it wasn't what she saw that touched her heart: it was what she felt. She felt safe and warm and welcome. She felt at home.

"May I take photographs?"

"Yes."

He waited while she walked around snapping pictures. After she had finished she slung her camera over her shoulder and went to stand by his side.

He reached for her hand. "Hannah...."

"Yes?"

He was silent a long time, and then he said, "Not yet...."

What had he been going to say? She waited, hoping he would change his mind.

Finally she said, "Are you ready to show me the drawings on the wall?"

"I'll start at the beginning." He turned the beam of light onto the wall nearest the entrance. "This is my calendar."

"May I photograph these as we go?"

"Yes."

Her heart hurt as she zoomed in on the marks that covered the walls. Amazing how the passage of twenty years could look when it was visible at a glance. Frightening. Lonely. Hopeless, even.

"All right," she said, and he shone the beam on the list of names he'd carved—his own name, the names of his parents and his wolf family, the name of his hometown.

"So I wouldn't forget." His words were stripped bare of everything except the stark truth.

Next he showed her the carvings. In sequence. His early carvings depicted day-to-day activities—hunting with the wolves, bathing in the river, sitting on a ridge underneath a full moon.

They became more sophisticated as the years went by, more detailed as he began to carve scenes that portrayed the passing of seasons and the social lives of his wolf family.

"Amazing," she said. "How did you get the colors?"

"Various ways. Some from ground roots and bark, others from powder hammered from the rocks."

Every inch of space on the walls was covered, from the ground to as high as he could reach. Hannah lost track of time as she snapped pictures of his incredible artwork.

When she was finished she was so emotionally drained she sat on an outcropping of stone. Hunter bent over her and softly caressed her hair. She turned her face up to his, and in that moment they might have come together as naturally as binary stars.

But Hunter stepped back and she reached into her backpack.

"Hungry?" she asked, and he accepted the beef jerky she offered.

They ate in silence, and then she said, "Is that all?"

"For now."

"You mean there are more cave drawings?"

"There is nothing more to see."

"Today?"

"For a while."

"How long?"

"I don't know," he said. "We'd better get back. It will be dark soon."

Hannah glanced toward the bearskin pallet. Her heart must have been in her eyes, for Hunter gave her one long look then began to gather her supplies.

She followed him back down the mountain to her campsite. Her tent looked forlorn sitting there in the dark all by itself. She shivered.

"I'll lend you a bearskin," he said.

"No thanks. I'll be fine."

"I'll see you in the morning?"

"Yes. I'll stay one more day."

They stood only a few inches apart without touching.

The moon slanted across his face, emphasizing the high cheekbones and silvery eyes.

"Sweet dreams, Hunter," she whispered.

He touched her hair, then vanished into the night.

Hunter kept watch over her throughout the lonely night. When the moon faded silver to make way for the sun, a great white wolf and his mate joined him.

The wolves stationed themselves on either side of Hunter, and he put a hand on each massive head.

"There she is," Hunter said. "My mate."

He felt the empathy that rose from the great hearts beating within the lupine breasts, and he stroked their fur.

"I know what you're thinking. Why is she alone in her tent while I'm alone in the woods?"

They licked his hands and their warm breaths fogged the air.

What had once been so simple was now extraordinarily complex.

"I can't ask her to be mine until I know who I am."

When Hannah emerged from her tent the next morning Hunter was waiting for her.

"You've been here all night, haven't you?" she asked.

"How did you know?"

"I felt your presence."

"Good." He took her backpack. "What do you want to see today?"

"Can I get close enough to the wolves to get some candid shots of you interacting with them?"

"Yes."

"I won't scare them away?"

"No. They trust me."

They climbed upward once more, and when they neared

the top of the ridge, Hunter said, "Let me go ahead and prepare the way."

He disappeared over the ridge and after a while reappeared and waved to her. Camera ready, she followed at a distance.

The scene she came upon took her breath away. Hunter was sitting in a circle of wolves, his arms around two massive beasts. Two others leaned against his shoulders, two had their heads on his lap and two lay curled at his feet.

If she hadn't seen the peaks of Mt. McKinley rising in the background and the wild tangle of forest that surrounded them, she might have thought he was in the midst of a petting zoo with tame wolves.

She photographed until late evening, always careful not to get too close, always mindful that she was a guest in an unusual family. When the light began to wane, she motioned Hunter.

"Thank you," she said. "Can you thank the wolves for me?"

"I already did."

He took her arm and as they headed back to camp she was vividly aware that her time with Hunter had almost run out.

"I will need at least a month here," he said, as if he had read her mind, and probably he had. "At the end of that time, I'll know."

Her connection with him was so strong she didn't have to ask questions. She understood his quest.

"I'll come back for you," she said. "May first."

"If you haven't finished your story in South America by then, I'll wait."

"Where?"

"In the cave."

"Yes."

"You can find it without my help?"

"Of course."

They reached her camp at sunset, and the lingering glow turned him into a sort of surreal god, part wolf, part man. She cupped his face.

"Hunter, I want you to choose me."

"I know."

"And if you don't, if you choose to stay, I don't think I can bear to face you. I don't think I'm strong enough to stand in front of you and hear you say, 'I'm not coming back.' Do you understand what I'm saying?"

"I understand, Hannah."

He wove his fingers through her hair, then cupping her head he drew her close. His mouth descended on hers, and the magic overtook them for a small eternity.

When he finally broke away, she whispered, "If the answer is no, leave me a sign."

"I will." He brushed her lips with his fingertips. "Take care, Hannah."

"You, too."

She went into her tent so she wouldn't have to watch him leave. Sitting in the middle with her eyes closed, she wrapped her arms around herself and remembered. Every exquisite detail of every moment she'd spent with him.

And when the galleon of a moon flooded her campsite with silver, Hannah went outside and built a big fire. Then she shed her clothes inside, wrapped a blanket around herself and took up her station beside the flames.

From a distance she felt the watchful silvery eyes. Smiling, she let the blanket slip apart as she began her erotic love play.

She was playing to win.

Chapter Forty-Two

Hunter stood on the ridge watching Hannah's plane wing south. Shading his eyes, he followed the silver and blue Baron until it merged with the pale sapphire skies.

Denali had never seemed more desolate. Solitude had never been lonelier.

He went back inside his cave and rifled through his duffle bag until he found what he wanted. His books. Perhaps he was a wilderness man, after all, but this time he would have his books. This time he would keep language alive.

He opened a slim volume of Emily Dickinson's poetry, but instead of reading he remembered his last picture of Hannah, the blanket sliding open and firelight flickering over her soft skin. The memory took hold and wouldn't let go.

He set the book aside and took out canvas and paints. Another luxury he'd decided to bring along.

"Some primitive I turned out to be," he said, as much to hear the sound of his own voice as to chastise himself.

With her memory fresh in his mind, he painted the first stroke on the canvas.

He painted for days, filling canvas after canvas with images of Hannah. He painted with the fervor of a man driven to madness by passion. Finally, he slumped exhausted onto the bearskin and slept.

When he woke up he didn't know if he'd slept twelve hours or twenty-four. Twenty-four or forty-eight.

He raced to his calendar on the wall and carved off one day. Or had it been two?

One day wouldn't make that much difference, but from now on he'd have to be vigilant. He had an appointment to keep with Hannah.

After Denali, Hannah sweltered in the jungle. *Good,* she thought. She needed the distraction. Even an unpleasant one.

She threw all her energies into her work, driving herself so she wouldn't have time to think. By the end of the first week she was so exhausted she could barely move, let alone think.

"At this rate I'm going to kill myself," she said.

No matter what she did, May first wouldn't come any sooner. She decided to pace herself, and when memories of Hunter stole through her mind, she decided to give herself permission to sit down and savor them, to dream about how it had been between them and how it might be again.

Between taking field notes for the story she would do on the disappearing rain forests, she began writing the rest of Hunter's story. She worked far into the night with only the glow of the moon and the sound of night birds deep in the jungle to keep her company.

* * *

His second week in Denali, Hunter left the relative comfort of his cave along with his books and his canvases, and joined the wolf pack two miles away in a high meadow where moose were plentiful. In order for his month in Denali to be a true test, he had to return to the wild completely.

His wolf brothers welcomed him without reservation. He had not stayed away long enough to become a stranger to them. He joined the hunt, and when the wolves separated a large bull from the herd, Hunter brought it down with one well-placed arrow.

They would all eat well for a while. He carved out a section of the flank for himself, and left the rest for them. Hunter stored his meat in a snowbank, and that evening when the pack gathered underneath the moon to celebrate their success, he joined them.

But his heart was not in it. His heart was somewhere in South America where a courageous woman was using her powerful pen to try and reverse another ecological disaster.

The day she wrapped up her story, Hannah was ecstatic. Excitement stole her appetite, and instead of eating she started packing her gear. She would leave for Denali tomorrow. A day early. That would give her an extra day in case bad weather forced her to stay overnight somewhere.

She hardly slept at all that night, and when she got up the next morning she thought her fatigue was due to sleeplessness. She grabbed a couple of bags, started toward the plane and blackness swamped her.

She woke up on the ground, sweat-drenched and dizzy. When she tried to stand up, her legs buckled.

"My God, what's happening to me?"

She lay there for a moment, willing herself not to pass

out. Gnats flew at her eyes and mosquitoes feasted on her arms. The sun was already nearing its zenith.

"I must have been out a couple of hours." The sound of her own voice was unfamiliar to her, the hoarse croak of a sick woman.

She couldn't lie there in the sun or she could add sunstroke to whatever ailed her. With superhuman effort, Hannah crawled to her tent and curled into her sleeping bag.

"Twenty-four-hour virus," she said before she fell into another sweat-soaked, fever-racked sleep.

It was dark when she woke again, and she fumbled around for her water bottle. Even if it hadn't been dark she would have had a hard time seeing, for a headache almost blinded her.

By morning she knew she had something more than a simple virus. With the last bit of strength she possessed, she found her cell phone and dialed Belle Rose.

Hunter put the last mark on his calendar two days early in case he'd miscalculated that long sleep he took the first week. Then he stepped outside his cave onto the newly greening grass and searched the skies for Hannah's plane.

Long into the night he watched, and finally he went to bed. She was too smart to try and fly into the wilderness in the dark. Besides, he was early.

The next day he took up his vigil again…then the day after that…and the day after that.

"Her work delayed her," he said, then he forced himself to sleep. He wanted to be in top form when Hannah arrived.

By the fifth day Hunter was getting worried. What if she'd hit bad weather? What if she'd crashed?

He berated himself for not bringing any way to communicate with him. Why hadn't he brought a cell phone? A radio? What had once seemed a simple test to discover who he was now seemed a rash and selfish act, fraught with stupidity.

Why hadn't he considered the possibility that Hannah might need him, or he might need her?

By the sixth day Hunter had decided that something terrible had happened to Hannah. The only way he would ever know would be to try and walk out.

But what if he left and Hannah had merely been delayed by work? What if she arrived and he was not there?

There was nothing to do except remain near the cave for a while longer.

The wolves, sensing his turmoil, came to stand sentinel beside him as he kept his lonely vigil.

Chapter Forty-Three

May 10, 2002

Hannah nearly scared us to death when she called from South America. She was so sick we could barely hear her. "Hang on, sweetheart," Michael told her. "I'm going to call a doctor and send him in, then I'll fly down to bring you home."

"Hurry, Dad," she said, and that was all.

Well, I acted a complete fool, blubbering and carrying on. "I can't lose her," I kept saying. "I nearly lost you and I can't lose her."

"Darling, we're not going to lose her. Hannah's one of the strongest people I know. She's a fighter. Just like her beautiful mom."

That got to me. It really did. Michael has always had a way of making me feel as if I'm some kind of prize catch, the woman he would choose even if he could pick from anybody in the world. And he could. Oh, he could. He's that magnificent.

Anyway...he hired a private plane to fly him into the jungle so he could fly Hannah back in hers. Lord, Hannah got all his grit and his talents...a lust for flying and adventuring, a lust for life.

By the time Michael got there, a local doctor had already responded to his call and was with Hannah. Michael said he was a young doctor, just out of medical school.

"Malaria," he told Michael. "Fortunately for your daughter, a very mild case."

Since the doctor was doing such a good job, Michael stayed a couple of days until Hannah was strong enough to travel.

Now she's in a hospital near Belle Rose, getting stronger every day and ornery as all get out.

Yesterday she told me, "I've got to get out of here even if I have to walk out without being dismissed."

And I said to her, "You will do no such thing. Hunter Wolfe is a genius. He'll figure out something's wrong. He'll be there waiting when you get there."

"What if he's not? What if his answer is no, and he's long gone and I never get another chance to see him?"

"Horsefeathers!" I said, and Hannah laughed so hard she got a stitch in her side.

It was strong laughter, too. After she'd got over her mirth she said, "They're starving me to death in here. Call Dad and tell him to bring me a double burger with french fries and a chocolate malted milk."

About that time Michael came in the door with this big smile on his gorgeous face and an armload of sacks from Burger King.

"With cheese, I hope," he said, and I said, "Michael

Westmoreland, I do believe you've added mind-reading to your many talents."

"So you think I have many talents, do you?"

He got this amazingly sexy look on his face, and of course I started flirting with him like crazy with Hannah egging me on from the bed. "Way to go, Mom. Strut your stuff."

I love that about Michael and me, that we still flirt with each other, and that we do it in front of our children so they can see for themselves what true love does to people. It never grows stale. It just gets better and better.

Clarice came in about that time bringing a sackful of creme-filled doughnuts. "Are you two at it again?" she said, then she gave this big dramatic sigh (typical Clarice-style). By that time Michael and I were kissing, mostly because we wanted to, but partially because we knew Hannah and Clarice were getting such a kick out of our shenanigans.

"A girl could starve to death waiting for these two lovebirds," Clarice said, and Hannah told her, "I don't intend to wait. I need my strength."

The two of them began ripping into sacks, and I swear to you, you could smell the calories.

All four of us sat on Hannah's bed laughing and carrying on and eating like pigs. It was one of those serendipitous times I will remember often and cherish always.

Chapter Forty-Four

She was fifteen days late. As Hannah set her plane down in Denali, excitement pulsed through her. And fear.

What if Hunter didn't come? What if he had given up and gone to another part of the vast parklands? What if he had followed the wolves to some faraway corner of the wilderness? One she would never find?

It was almost dark when she landed, far too late to go trekking up the mountain in search of Hunter's cave.

She unloaded her gear and set up her tent, all the while searching the woods for any signs of him. By the time she had finished setting up camp, she was exhausted.

Her mother had thought it was too soon to come, that she needed to wait another week in order to be stronger. But Michael had said, "It's all right, Anne. Hannah wouldn't be leaving unless she knew she could make it."

Her dad had been right. She'd known she could make

the long trip. In order to see Hunter again, she would walk through fire and flood.

A sound caught her attention. A twig snapping? A footstep on the forest floor?

Hannah whirled toward the deep woods and squinted into the gathering darkness. There was nothing except the long shadows of trees.

She ate beans cold out of the can and drank plenty of water, then fell into her sleeping bag with the thought that he might come to her at night, that he might stand watch from a distance for old time's sake.

She woke up at dawn and, wrapping a quilt around herself, hurried outside. There was no sign of him. If he had come during the night, she hadn't heard him. Her sleep had been too deep.

It was almost sunset when Hunter heard the light plane. He and the wolf pack were miles away in a high mountain meadow, teaching two young wolves to hunt small game. The two youngsters had chased rabbits all day without any success, and the leader of the pack was chastising them for not taking their lesson seriously.

The resulting squabble was so loud that at first Hunter wasn't certain of what he'd heard. He raced across the meadow, scrambled to the top of a bluff and strained his eyes upward. There. A tiny silver speck.

As the plane came closer, the droning of the engine grew louder. Was it Hannah? At this distance it was impossible to tell.

Hunter didn't wait for confirmation. He couldn't wait.

His heart hammering, he set out running. If he paced himself he would be back at his cave by morning.

Everything looked different clothed in green. Was she on the right trail? Hannah wasn't going to start second-guessing herself. If she did she would lose confidence, and perhaps even lose her way.

She climbed steadily upward, stopping every now and then to catch her breath. While she rested she wished all sorts of calamities on the disease-carrying mosquito that had temporarily robbed her of her stamina.

In spite of her frequent rest stops, she arrived at the cave shortly after sunrise. Hannah let out a whoop and raced toward the mouth. Dense growth made a green curtain that almost obscured the opening.

''Hunter?''

She called his name and waited for a response. There was nothing except a vast and empty silence. Should she go in or wait outside?

Wait, she decided. ''Hunter? Are you there?''

Why would he be waiting in the cave after two weeks? It was too much to hope for.

''I'm not going to panic,'' she said, then she sat down on a medium-size boulder to wait.

Perhaps he had gone to the stream to bathe. Or maybe he was out hunting. There were any number of reasons why Hunter was not there.

Time inched by. Hannah tipped her canteen up and took a long drink of water.

What if something had happened to him? Something terrible? Or what if he had decided to remain in the wilderness? What if his answer was no?

Leaving her backpack beside the cave, she skirted the area looking for a sign. Hadn't he said he'd leave her a sign? Hadn't she said, *If you choose to stay, I don't think I can bear to face you.*

What sort of sign would he leave? Obviously it would be near the cave. Or perhaps even inside.

She had to go in. Taking her flashlight from her backpack, she knelt in front of the opening and pushed the curtain of tangled vines aside.

"Hannah...."

Suddenly he was there. She looked up into the amazing silver eyes, and lost her breath.

"Is it really you?" he said, then knelt beside her and caught her shoulders. "I can't believe it...." He traced her eyebrows, her cheekbones, her lips. She wanted to revel in his touch forever.

"I thought you weren't going to come," she whispered.

"I'll always come to you, Hannah. No matter what."

He didn't ask why she was late. He didn't ask for explanations. He merely devoured her with his incredible eyes.

"If you hadn't come, I was going to walk out of the wilderness to find you," he said.

Yes, she exulted. *Yes! Sometimes the angels smile.*

She held her breath, drowning in him. "Come," he said, and she followed him into the mouth of his cave.

It was colder inside the thick rock cavern, and when the ceiling opened up, she wrapped her arms around herself, shivering. Hunter pulled her into a warm embrace and held her for a very long time. They didn't talk, didn't move; they absorbed each other.

At last Hunter said, "I have something to show you, Hannah."

He led her to a far corner of the cave, then holding her from behind, he turned the beam of her flashlight onto the wall. The last of the cave drawings ended, and a large block of text began.

It was a while before Hannah could make sense of what she saw, and then she began to make out the words. "How do I love thee? Let me count the ways...."

It was all there, every word of Elizabeth Barrett Browning's love sonnet.

"I started carving that about a year after the crash," he said, reading her mind. "It was the poem my father quoted to my mother."

"Amazing."

She fell silent as he read the rest of the sonnet aloud. She imagined him as a young boy chipping away at the rock, bit by laborious bit preserving a part of his past.

"I was afraid I would forget," he said. "I was afraid the wilderness would steal my memory of and my capacity for love."

He tightened his hold on her. "In a way, it did. As the years went by I stopped reading the sonnet, and then the memory of words faded altogether. Along with the memory of that kind of love."

She felt the tension in him, the passion. But there was something so sacred, so beautiful about his confession that she didn't want to interrupt. Hardly daring to breath, she waited.

"When you first came to Denali, I was more wolf than man...but you loved me anyhow. You gave yourself freely to me, Hannah, nothing held back, nothing required.

"You gave it all back to me," he added, "the words, the memory. But most of all love." He turned her in his arms and cupped her face. "I love you, Hannah, and I want to be with you for the rest of my life if you'll have me."

It was more than she'd ever hoped for, more than she'd dreamed. If he had said, "I want to mate with you for the rest of my life," she'd have been happy. But to have love, too, was almost overwhelming.

In spite of her independence, in spite of her free-wheeling lifestyle, she'd had a secret dream all her life: to find the kind of love her parents had. Never mind all the trappings. She just wanted the love.

"Yes," she said. "I'll not only have you, I'll follow you to the ends of the earth. Wherever you are, whatever you want to be, I'll be there at your side. Loving you, Hunter. Always loving you."

He picked her up and carried her to the bearskin pallet, and there, surrounded by the evidence of his life as a wolfman, they came together as a man and a woman who truly love.

Chapter Forty-Five

July 20, 2002

Last week I became grandmother to the most beautiful baby in the world. Michael agrees, so that's a majority opinion, not the biased blatherings of two doting grandparents.

Jake called us in the middle of the night and said, "I'm taking Emily to the hospital. Your granddaughter is on her way."

Michael grabbed the pink teddy bear and I grabbed the pink hand-crocheted receiving blanket and off we went. In Michael's plane.

"Pity the poor grandparents who have to fight traffic," he said.

"Or fly commercial," I added.

Oh, we were so proud of ourselves. It wasn't until we got to Atlanta that we remembered our luggage. Sitting in the bedroom closet where it had been packed and ready to go for two weeks.

My darling husband and I looked at each other and cracked up.

"I prefer you without clothes anyway," he told me, and I said, "You're acting mighty spry for an old grandpa."

We caught a cab from the airport and cracked grandpa/grandma jokes all the way to the hospital. By the time we got there, Emily was in the pushing mode, and we paced the hall like any two sane first-time grandparents.

Every five minutes Michael said to me, "Do you think Emily's all right?" and I said, "Darling, women have been having babies since the beginning of time. Our daughter is going to come through like a champ."

At times like that it's wonderful to belong to the sisterhood of women, to be the keeper of secrets, the oracle of wisdom.

While we waited, Michael drank so much coffee that I told him, "You're going to be up all night." He gave me an incredibly sexy, for-my-eyes-only look and said, "Good."

Lord, it's a sight how this amazing man can ring my chimes. And me a grandmother.

Of course, Michael and I had already discussed our new status.

"We'll love the baby with all our hearts," Michael told me, "but she will belong to Emily and Jake. The three of them will be a core family."

"That's the way it should be," I said.

"Being grandparents will not change us," he told me. "Our relationship will still always be first."

Call me selfish, but his declaration thrilled me all the

way to my bones. Actually, call me the luckiest woman alive.

When I think of all the otherwise sane people who turn their lives upside-down in order to devote themselves exclusively to a child, it makes me realize how very lucky I am. I've even seen people who can barely stand each other, remain chained together because of progeny.

How sad. How tragic.

Life should be lived fully, with arms and heart wide open.

Anyway, back to our escapades in Atlanta....

By the time our nerves were thoroughly frayed, Jake stepped into the hall with a huge grin on his face and announced, "I have a son."

"You mean a daughter, don't you?" I said, because naturally I thought the stress of childbirth had addled him.

"No, I mean a boy! Come inside and meet Jacob Michael."

Oh, the look on Michael's face! Priceless.

We went inside and Jake laid the baby in Michael's arms. That's the first time he's cried since he came out of the coma.

The beautiful thing about my precious husband's tears is that he's not afraid of letting his feelings show.

"Look at the size of those hands," he said. "And those feet. He's going to be a fine mountain climber."

"Or a great concert pianist," I said, and when Michael handed the baby to me he said, "Another musician in this family would be wonderful."

See why I love this man so.

Daniel and Skylar came to see the baby, and I could tell what they were thinking by the way they looked at each other. It wouldn't surprise me if they start their family soon.

We left them with Emily and Jake while we raced to Rich's and bought out the baby department. "My grandson's not going home from the hospital in pink," Michael said.

After our spree we checked into a hotel sans luggage, and got some funny looks.

"Let's relax awhile before we call Hannah," Michael said, so we stripped off our clothes and crawled into bed and you know where that led. Thank goodness.

Afterward we held each other close and Michael said, "You know what I was thinking the whole time we were in the hospital?"

"No. What?"

"How I could hardly wait to make love to you." He kissed me, and one thing led to another.

It was dark before we called Hannah. On her cell phone.

She and Hunter are in Denali "living wild and free" as she puts it.

I've never seen her happier. She and Hunter are so much in love. He returned with her in May. They stayed at her cottage in the woods for a few weeks.

"I'm regaining my strength and Hunter's painting," she told me after they got back from Denali.

"Then what?" I asked her, and she said, "I'm going to the Everglades on assignment in June. Hunter will go with me. He'll paint while I'm working. He's getting ready for another show in October."

"And after that?"

"If you're listening for wedding bells, Mom, you can forget it."

I guess I was, in a way, but knowing Hannah, I should have expected the unusual.

"Not really," I told her. "I only want you to be happy, Hannah, and secure in that happiness. That's all."

"I'm very, very happy and completely secure. Don't you know, Mom? Wolves mate for life."

Hannah loves to shock, but I have news for her. I'm not a bit shocked. I'm ecstatic. They love each other, and people who love each other should be together. Period. End of discussion.

The lifestyle they've worked out is totally unconventional, which is exactly the way it should be with two people as unusual as Hannah and Hunter.

After they came back from the Everglades, they loaded up Hannah's plane and flew back to Denali.

"We plan to spend all our summers there," she told me. "Living wild and free."

And though she didn't say as much, I suspect that "living wild and free" means that for a brief interlude each summer she will become wolfwoman to Hunter's wolfman.

It almost makes me wish I were young again.

But then I wouldn't have what I do. This remarkable love that came through a six-month fire of separation stronger and more beautiful than ever.

Hannah and Hunter will be back in time for Jacob Michael's christening in September.

So will Clarice. She and Larry Baird are in Italy.

I halfway expected this to be a honeymoon, but then knowing Clarice, I'm not surprised that she's still putting off a wedding. Larry asked her to marry him six times before she ever accepted a ring, but she won't even talk about a wedding date.

"We're having too much fun to stop so some old fogey with a degree can sanction us," she said.

Oh, it will be good to have everybody gathered at Belle Rose once more. The entire family, plus a few good friends.

Afterward Michael and I are going to Italy. "Nowhere near the Dolomites," he assured me, and I said, "Thank you, darling."

Then I finally told him the truth. "I don't think I could bear to see you near another mountain. They stole six months from us, and I won't ever risk that again."

"You won't have to, my precious. I don't plan ever to leave your side."

Italy is going to be wonderful. "A second honeymoon," Michael said, and we both laughed.

But our time in Italy is so much more than a second honeymoon. It's a fulfillment of the promise we made to each other...to keep our relationship sacred.

We will wrap ourselves in a pink cocoon, and there we will stay, loving each other till the end of time...and beyond.

Chapter Forty-Six

Nature compensated the frozen Northwest by turning it into a lush blooming Eden in summertime. In the midst of this rainbow-hued paradise in the remote reaches of Denali, Hunter and Hannah cavorted like a naughty Adam and Eve.

They raced from their cave and through the wilderness to a mirror-smooth lake so clear they could see their reflections.

"Last one in is a rotten egg," Hannah yelled, then executed a perfect dive into the water.

Hunter sliced the surface nearby, and grabbing her by the ankle pulled her under for a long, watery kiss.

"How long has it been since I mated with you?" he asked when they surfaced.

"About an hour."

"That's far too long."

Wrapping her legs around his waist, Hunter plunged into

her with the lust of a man who never ceased to be aroused
by the sight of the woman he loved.

"Yes, yes, *yes*." Her pleasure-cries bounced off the
bluffs and echoed back across the lake.

Water swirled and rippled around them as they came
together, time and again.

"I can't get enough of you," he said. "I can never get
enough of you."

He scooped her out of the water and climbed up a rocky
incline as if she weighed no more than a baby. Water roared
around them, the thundering cascade of a waterfall.

With the assurance of a man familiar with his terrain,
Hunter carried her across a narrow ledge and behind the
curtain of water.

"Where are we going?" she said.

"You'll see."

Suddenly the rock wall disappeared and they stood in a
cavernous opening.

"It's a cave!"

"Yes," he said. "A secret love bower."

As he walked inside the cool cavern, Hannah felt like a
bride being carried across the threshold. It didn't strike her
as the least bit odd that she thought of such an analogy.

She was Hunter's mate as surely as if they'd stood in the
grandest cathedral in the world and pledged vows before a
crowd of thousands.

The cave was smaller than the one where they sum-
mered—cozier. Sunlight poured through a large natural
skylight, and underneath lay a pallet of fur.

"Surprise," Hunter said.

"Amazing," she whispered, but then why should she be
amazed? Each day with Hunter was like discovering life
anew. Each moment was a precious gift. Each time they
loved, magic.

As she looked at the pallet she remembered the first time they had mated…in the leaves beside the Mississippi River. That it had happened at all between two people who couldn't even talk to each other was a miracle.

A miracle that had repeated itself time and again.

A miracle she longed to recreate today.

Positioning her on the pallet, Hunter thrust deep inside. And as his love cry echoed off the walls, Hannah understood that their communication had never needed words.

She and her wolfman communicated with their hearts.

The cave resounded with the joyful sounds of their mating, and when they finally emerged, the sinking sun was setting the heavens afire.

"Look, Hannah."

She looked not at the sky, but at the gathering of wolves on the shore.

"Did they come to drink?"

"No, they came for the ceremony."

"What ceremony?"

"You'll see."

He led her underneath the curtain of water and down the rocky path to the water's edge.

"Hold my hand, Hannah, and don't let go."

As they joined hands, a dozen massive heads turned their way. A dozen pairs of yellow eyes watched.

Hunter lifted their joined hands high. "My brothers, this is the woman I have chosen to be my mate. She is Hannah, alpha female."

The wolves stood at attention with their ears pricked and intelligence shining from their eyes. It didn't matter whether they understood his words; they understood his heart.

"From this day forward she is Wolfe's woman. Welcome her into the pack."

A large white wolf separated himself from the pack and came slowly forward. Holding her breath, Hannah read Hunter's thoughts as clearly as if he had spoken aloud.

Don't move. Be still.

The wolf brushed against her leg, then positioned himself beside her. He stood facing the other wolves for a moment, then slowly he moved his large muzzle toward Hannah's hand.

As the large mouth closed over her hand, she willed herself to stillness. The wolf held her in a surprisingly gentle grasp, and when she felt a small tug, Hunter said, ''Go with him, Hannah.''

The wolf led her toward the rest of the pack. They waited until the great white male released her hand, and then one by one they rubbed themselves against her legs. Instinctively, she leaned down and put one hand on the head of the white male.

''Welcome to the pack,'' Hunter said.

And then her magnificent wolfman joined her in the circle of his brothers.

*   *   *   *   *

*Silhouette presents an exciting
new continuity series:*

**When a royal family rolls out the red carpet
for love, power and deception, will their
lives change forever?**

The saga begins in April 2002 with:

The Princess Is Pregnant!

by Laurie Paige (SE #1459)

**May: THE PRINCESS AND THE DUKE by Allison Leigh
(SE #1465)**

**June: ROYAL PROTOCOL by Christine Flynn
(SE #1471)**

Be sure to catch all nine Crown and Glory stories: the first three appear in
Silhouette Special Edition, the next three continue in Silhouette Romance
and the saga concludes with three books in Silhouette Desire.

───────────────

And be sure not to miss more royal stories,
from Silhouette Intimate Moments'

Romancing
the Crown,

running January through December.

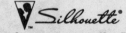

Coming in May 2002

**Three Bravo men marry for convenience—
but will they love in leisure? Find out in
Christine Rimmer's *Bravo Family Ties!***

Cash—for stealing a young woman's innocence, and to
give their baby a name, in *The Nine-Month Marriage*

Nate—for the sake of a codicil in his beloved
grandfather's will, in *Marriage by Necessity*

Zach—for the unlucky-in-love rancher's chance to
have a marriage—even of convenience—
with the woman he *really* loves!

BRAVO
FAMILY TIES

Where love comes alive™